Dear Readers,

I still remember the first time I read Donald Goines, the godfather of street lit. He was the first to write books about characters I could identify with. To some, the stories may have been aggressive, overly stylized, and even dangerous. But there was an honesty there—a realness. I made a vow that if I wrote a book or got into the publishing game, I would try the same one-two punch—that of a *Daddy Cool* or *Black Gangster*.

After the success of my *New York Times* bestselling memoir, *From Pieces to Weight*, I rounded up some of the top writers, same way I rounded up some of the top rappers in the game, to form **G Unit** and take this series to the top of the literary world. The stories from **G Unit** are the kinds of dramas me and my crew have been dealing with our whole lives: death, deceit, double-crosses, ultimate loyalty, and total betrayal. It's about our life on the streets, and no one knows it better than us. Not to mention, when it comes to authentic gritty urban stories of the high and low life, our audience expects the best. In *Derelict*, street lit superstar **Relentless Aaron** delivers a powerful portrait of a "relentless" ex-con collecting some payback. It's a reading experience I guarantee you won't forget.

You know, I don't do anything halfway. These may be works of fiction, but they tell the *truth* about life on The Street. Are you ready?

DERELICT

50 Cent
and Relentless Aaron

G Unit Books

NEW YORK   LONDON   TORONTO   SYDNEY   NEW DELHI

Pocket Books
A Division of Simon & Schuster, Inc.
1230 Avenue of the Americas
New York, NY 10020

First Pocket Books paperback edition November 2013

POCKET and colophon are registered trademarks of
Simon & Schuster, Inc.

For information about special discounts for bulk purchases,
please contact Simon & Schuster Special Sales at 1-866-506-1949
or business@simonandschuster.com.

The Simon & Schuster Speakers Bureau can bring authors to your
live event. For more information or to book an event contact the
Simon & Schuster Speakers Bureau at 1-866-248-3049 or visit our
website at www.simonspeakers.com.

Manufactured in the United States of America

10 9 8 7 6 5 4 3 2 1

ISBN 978-1-4767-3484-2
ISBN 978-1-4165-5969-6 (ebook)

Dedication

To those of whom little was expected but who achieved much; to those who ever turned their lemons into lemonade; and to the discouraged, the oppressed, the misled and the misunderstood souls who are otherwise known as worthless, useless or unproductive. . . .

This book is dedicated to you. Please know that it is possible to overcome the challenges, but when you do succeed, realize that struggle never stops surfacing. Therefore, you must enjoy living and make the best of your life *regardless* of your circumstances. Failure is but one more step toward accomplishment. I am living proof that you can win, especially if you stick to it and give it your all. So, to everyone that reads this, get off your butt and win. **But win big!**

To my children, I love you and I work hard so that you may live a better life. To Julie and Wataani, Tiny, Shetalia, and the rest of the Relentless team, stay true and thank you so much. To Allyson (Jama's momma), thanks for having my back on this and other books. And Alise, I wouldn't know them without knowing you. You are a strong pillar in my life. I intend to be the same for you. My unconditional love to all of you.

Finally, to all of those **Relentless Readers** from around the world, thank you for your total support on this project! Thank you for supporting me from book one to book one thousand. Only you know true talent when you see it. You're savvy, voracious, tireless readers, and I work hard to satisfy you. Thank you for overcoming the shallow critics and carrying me from the bottom to the top. **We did it! One and all!**

Love, Peace & Happiness,
Relentless Aaron

DERELICT: shamefully negligent in not having done what one should have done.

DERELICT

CHAPTER 1

Prison: **One of the few places on earth where sharks sleep, and where "you reap what you sow."**

The note that prisoner Jamel Ross attached with his (so-called) urgent request to see the prison psycho-therapist was supposed to appear desperate: "I need to address some serious issues because all I can think about is killing two people when I leave here. Can you help me!" And that's all he wrote. But, even more than the anger, revenge, and redemption Jamel was ready to bring back to the streets, he also had the prison's psych as a target; a target of his lust. And that was a more pressing issue at the moment.

- - - -

"As far back as I can remember life has been about growing pains," he told her. "I've been through the phases of a liar in my adolescence, a hustler and thug in my teens, and an all-out con man in my twenties. Maybe it was just my instincts to acquire what I considered resources—by whatever means necessary—but it's a shame that once you get away with all of those behaviors, you become good at it, like some twisted type of talent or profession. Eventually even lies feel like the truth . . .

"I had a good thing going with *Superstar*. The magazine. The cable television show. Meeting and commingling with the big-name celebrities and all. I was positioned to have the biggest multimedia company in New York, the biggest to focus on black entertainment exclusively. BET was based in Washington at the time, so I had virtually no competition. Jamel Ross, the big fish in a little pond . . .

"And of course I got away with murder, figuratively, when Angel—yes, the singer with the TV show and all her millions of fans—didn't go along with the authorities, including her mother, who wanted to hit me with child molestation, kidnapping, and other charges. I was probably dead wrong for laying with that girl before she turned eighteen. But Angel was a very grown-up seventeen-year-old. Besides, when I hit it she was only a few months shy from legal. So gimme a break.

"In a strange way, fate came back to get my ass for all of my misdeeds. All of my pimpmania. That cable company up in Connecticut, with more than four hundred stations and fifty-five million subscribers across the country, was purchased by an even larger entity. It turned my life around when that happened; made my brand-new, million-dollar contract null and void. There was no way that I could sue anyone because lawyers' fees are incredible and my company over-extended itself with the big celebrations, the lavish spending, and the increased staff; my living expenses, including the midtown penthouse, the car notes, and maintenance for Deadra and JoJo—my two lovers at the time—were in excess of eleven thousand a month. Add that to the overhead at *Superstar* and, without a steady stream of cash flowing, I had an ever-growing monster on my hands.

"One other thing, both Deadra and JoJo became pregnant, so now I would soon have four who depended on me as the sole provider. Funny, all of this wasn't an issue when things were lean. When the sex was good and everyone was kissing my ass. Now, I'm the bad guy because the company's about to go belly-up."

■ ■ ■ ■

With a little more than two years left to his eighty-four-month stretch, Jamel Ross finally got his wish, to sit and spill his guts to Dr. Kay Edmondson, the psychotherapist at Fort Dix—the federal correctional institution that was a fenced-in forty-acre plot on that much bigger Fort Dix Army Base. Fort Dix was where army reservists came to train, and simultaneously where felons did hard time for crimes gone wrong. With so many unused acres belonging to the government during peacetime, someone imagined that perhaps a military academy or some other type of income-producing entity would work on Fort Dix, as well. So they put a prison there.

The way that Fort Dix was set up was very play it by ear. It was a growing project where rules were implemented along the way. Sure, there was a Bureau of Prisons guidebook with rules and regulations for both staff and convicts to follow. However, that BOP guidebook was very boilerplate, and it left the prison administrators in a position in which they had to learn to cope and control some three thousand offenders inside the fences of what was the largest population in the federal system. It was amazing how it all stayed intact for so long.

"On the pound" nicknames were appreciated and accepted since it was a step away from a man's birth name, or "government name," which was the name that all the corrections officers, administrative staff, and of course, the courts used when addressing convicts. So on paper Jamel's name was Jamel Ross. On paper, Jamel Ross was not considered to be a person, but a convict with the registration number 40949–054, something like the forty-thousandth prisoner to be filtered through the Southern District of New York. The "054" ending was a sort of area code in his prison ID number. He was sentenced by Judge Benison in October of 1997 and committed to eighty-four months—no parole, and three years probation. The conviction was for bank robbery. However, on appeal, the conviction was "adjusted" since there was no conclusive evidence that Jamel had a weapon. Nevertheless, Jamel certainly *did* have a weapon and fully intended to pull off a robbery, with a pen as his weapon. So the time he was doing was more deserved than not.

But regardless of Jamel's level of involvement, it was suddenly very easy for him to share himself since he felt he had nothing to lose. It was that much easier to speak to a reasonably attractive woman, as if there were good reasons for the things he did. So he went on explaining all of his dirty deeds to "Dr. Kay" Edmondson as if this were a confessional where he'd be forgiven for his sins. And why not? She was a good-listening, career-oriented female. She was black and she wasn't condescending like so many other staff members were. And when she called him "Jamel," as opposed to "Convict Ross," it made him imagine they had a tighter bond in store.

"So this dude—I won't say his name—he let me in on his check game. He explained how one person could write a check for, say, one hundred grand, give it to a friend, and even if the money isn't there to back up the check, the depositor could likely withdraw money on it before it is found to be worthless. It sounded good. And I figured the worst-case scenario would be to deny this and to deny that . . ."

"They don't verify the check? I mean, isn't that like part of the procedure before it clears?" Kay generally did more talking than this when convicts sat before her. Except she was finding his story, as well as his in-depth knowledge of things, so fascinating.

"See, that's the thing. If the check comes from the same region, or if it's from the other side of the world, it still has to go through a clearing house, where all of the checks from *all* of the banks eventually go. So that takes like a couple of days. But banks—certain banks—are on some ol' 'we trust you' stuff, and I guess since they've got your name and address and stuff, they do the cash within one or two days."

"Really?"

"Yup. They will if it's a local check from a local bank. And on that hundred grand? The bank will let loose on the second day. I'll go in and get the money when the dam breaks . . ."

"And when the bank finds out about the check being no good?"

"I play dumb. I don't know the guy who wrote the check. Met him only twice, blah blah blah. I sign this little BS affidavit and *bang*—I'm knee-deep in free money."

Dr. Kay wagged her head of flowing hair and replied, "You all never cease to amaze me. I mean *you*, as in the convicts here. I hear all sorts of tricks and shortcuts and—"

"Cons. They're cons, Dr. Kay."

"Sure, sure . . ." she somehow agreed.

"But it's all a dead end, ya know? Like, once you get money, it becomes an addiction, to the point that you forget your *reasons* and *objectives* for getting money in the first place."

"Did *you* forget, Jamel?"

"Did I? I got *so deep* in the whole check thing that it became my new profession."

"Stop playin'."

"I'm for real. I started off with my own name and companies, but then, uh . . ." Jamel hesitated. He looked away from the doctor. "I shouldn't really be tellin' you this. I'm ramblin'."

"You don't have to if you don't want to, but let me remind you that what you say to me in our sessions is confidential, unless I feel that you might cause harm to yourself or someone else, or if I'm subpoenaed to testify in court."

"Hmmm." Jamel deliberated on that. He wondered if the eighty-four-month sentence could be enhanced to double or triple, or worse. He'd heard about the nightmares, how bragging while in prison was a tool that another prisoner could use to shorten his own sentence. "Informants" they called them. And just the *thought* of that made Jamel promise himself that he wouldn't say a thing about the weapon and the real reason he caught so much time.

"Off the record, Jamel . . ."

"Oooh, I like this 'off-the-record' stuff." Jamel rubbed his hands together and came to the edge of the couch from his slouched position.

"Well, to put your mind at ease, I haven't yet received a subpoena for a trial."

Jamel took that as an indication of secrecy and that he was supposed to have confidence in her. But he proceeded with caution as he went on explaining about the various bank scams, the phony licenses, and bogus checks.

The doctor said, "Wow, Jamel. That's a hell of a switch. One day you're a television producer, a publisher, and a ladies' man, and the next—"

The phone rang.

"I'm sorry." Dr. Kay got up from her chair, passed

9

Jamel, and circled her desk. It gave him a whiff of her perfume and that only made him pay special attention to her calves. There was something about a woman's calves that got him excited. Or didn't. But Dr. Kay's calves *did*. As she took her phone call, Jamel wondered if she did the StairMaster bit, or if she ran in the mornings. Maybe she was in the military like most of these prison guards claimed. Was she an aerobics instructor at some point in her life? All of those ideas were flowing like sweet Kool-Aid in Jamel's head as he thought and wondered and imagined.

"Could you excuse me?" Dr. Kay said.

"Sure," said Jamel, and he quickly stepped out of the office and shut the door behind him. Through the door's window he tried to cling to her words. It seemed to be a business call, but that was just a guess. A hope. It was part of Jamel's agenda to guess and wonder what this woman or that woman would be like underneath him, or on top of him. After all, he was locked up and unable to touch a female being. So his imaginings were what had guided him during these years. He'd take time to look deep into a woman, and those thoughts weren't frivolous but anchored and supported by his past. Indeed, sex had been a major part of his life since he was a teen. It had become a part of his lifestyle. Women. The fine ones. The ones who weren't so fine, but whom he felt he could "shape up and get right." Dr. Kay was somewhere in between those images. She had a cute face and an open attitude. Her eyes smiled large and compassionate. She was cheeky when she smiled, with lips wide and supple. Her teeth were bright and indicated good hygiene.

And Dr. Kay wasn't built like an *Essence* model or a dancer in a video. She was a little thick where it mattered, and she had what Jamel considered to be "a lot to work with." Big-breasted and with healthy hips, Dr. Kay was one of a half dozen women on the compound who were black. There were others who were Hispanic and a few more who were white. But of those who were somehow accessible, Dr. Kay nicely fit Jamel's reach. And to reach her, all he had to do was make the effort to trek on down to the psychology department, in the same building as the chapel and the hospital. All you had to do was express interest in counseling. Then you had to pass a litmus test of sorts, giving your reason for needing counseling. Of course, Dr. Kay wasn't the only psychotherapist in the department. There were one or two others. So Jamel had to hope and pray 1) that his interview would be with Dr. Kay Edmondson, and 2) that his address would be taken sincerely, not as just another sex-starved convict who wanted a whiff or an eyeful of the available female on the compound.

Considering all of that, Jamel played his cards right and was always able to have Dr. Kay set him up for a number of appointments. It couldn't be once a week; the doctor-convict relationship would quickly burn out at that rate. But twice a month was a good start, so that she could get a grip on who (and what) he was about. Plus, his visits wouldn't be so obvious as to raise any red flags with her boss, who, as far as Jamel could tell, really didn't execute any major checks and balances on Kay's caseload. Still, it was the other prisoners at Fort Dix who Jamel had to be concerned about. They had to be outsmarted at every twist and turn, since they were the very people (miserable, locked-up, and jealous) who would often jump to conclusions. Any one of these guys might get the notion, the hint, or the funny idea that Dr. Kay was getting too personal with one prisoner. Then the dime dropping and the investigation would begin.

From where Dr. Kay sat, there were similar concerns. You never knew with these guys. Prisoners were nothing but crabs in a barrel, all of them waiting their turn to get out, or to get eaten alive. And who knew what they were thinking deep down in their conscience, or what their motives were. Sure, she imagined that somewhere in their minds there was the thought of sex and that they'd desire her at some point or another. But she also considered that to be normal and human. And wasn't that her profession as a prison psychotherapist? To help men deal with such issues? And with that, wasn't there the danger, the intrigue, and a whole lot of head cases? This kind of thing came with the territory. So she accepted it.

"So . . . where were we?" Dr. Kay asked when the call was finished and the convict was back in the office with the door shut for privacy.

"I was tellin' you my dirt."

"Oh yeah," she said, then sort of chuckled. "I just . . . I'm just amazed at how you could go from one extreme to the next. At one point, so it seems, you're on top of the world. The next, you're practically sticking up banks with a pen instead of a gun."

After the peculiar silence, Jamel said, "Sounds pretty sick, huh?"

"And if you don't mind me saying, *stupid*."

There was some more silence as Jamel looked down through his clasped hands.

Reality check, he thought.

Jamel raised his head and when he did she got to see something else; something new and different. Was this a tear forming? Okay . . .

The crying wasn't what was unique; Lord knows she had witnessed these guys crying over and over again. Even if they came in and acted like they were hard, she could generally see through their act and almost count the minutes until the floodgates opened. But Jamel was different, indeed. There was something very real about Jamel; very basic and uncharacteristic. It seemed as if he was but so far from having the world in his hands, a world of awareness, of intelligence, and of control. Whereas most of the men were at a loss for some definition, direction, and sense of conviction in their lives, Jamel seemed to have all of that. Why did he fail? She was trying to dig for that knowledge. But his heart was one of the unconquerable ones. It was why Jamel appeared to be so "unchained" in this prison community, where everything else (including a man's thoughts) was on twenty-four-hour lockdown. Jamel wasn't the thug he thought he was; just a man with a bold, risk-taking, fearless heart.

With that trembling voice, Jamel offered, "Under the circumstances, I did the best that I could. The best that *I knew how*. I got caught up in a black hole of responsibilities, people who depended on me. My dream slipped out from under my nose. Everything . . ." The tears flowed now. "It was all lost. Here I am paying my so-called debt to society, trying to get myself right. I'm stressed out, I'm fighting for my life with other men . . . we act like thugs, goons, and gangsters all day. We're all actin' hard in here; wearin' it like a bulletproof vest, even in the shower. And we gotta do it like this twenty-four/seven . . . and . . . and then I come here for . . . for someone to listen and counsel me and you can just *slam me like this*? I'm *stupid*? I'm some goddamn *freak* to you? I'm not even *human* to you, huh? I can't make a mistake. I'm not under some major pain in my life? Do you have any compassion?"

The doctor tried to cut in a few times. Tried to right this wrong situation. But Jamel kept going on. She could feel herself becoming remorseful, feeling more compassion, but maybe it was too late for that.

"I can't believe you could hurt me like this," Jamel continued as he pulled a couple of tissues from the box on the table between them. There was a book there near the box, its brilliant green cover showing off atop the polished pine box. *Black Firsts,* the book was titled. It was a book that Jamel had flipped through before when the doctor took quicker phone calls, when she *didn't* excuse him from the office. Jamel blew his nose and there was time enough for her to jump in.

"I'm . . . I apologize if I've hurt your feelings, I never meant to . . . I'm just . . . how do you say . . . 'keepin' it real' with you."

Dr. Kay watched as Jamel peeked up at her beyond his tears and the emotional turbulence that he showed. This had to be a first for him, too, to see the human side of her; to see that under all of the schooling, the training, and the experience with convicts that Dr. Kay Edmondson was merely Kay *the woman*. It was as close as she'd come to showing herself naked to a prisoner.

Wow, thought Jamel. This is *working*! It's *actually working*! Up until now, Jamel merely wanted to spend time with the woman, a black woman who could feel him and understand him and acknowledge his faults. Up until now, Dr. Kay was nothing less than an alternative in a community of men who had to jerk off in place of sex, or else lift weights to release tension. She was his outlet for relief, and his only connection to having a life on the streets. Essentially, speaking to Dr. Kay was an escape. It was freedom. But now there was more, and Jamel knew that what his heart was saying was the truth, even if he was doing a little extra acting. He'd had his way with women time and again back home in New York, so he could measure and assess just as well in prison. In here, even competing with the many fakes, phonies, and frauds who had no doubt walked through Dr. Kay's door with ulterior motives, Jamel suddenly saw possibility. And he couldn't be a hundred percent sure, but if he had to take a gamble, his bet was on the forthcoming, far-fetched physical relationship he would soon have with Dr. Kay Edmondson.

CHAPTER 2

Charm. That's what a lot of these convicts displayed during interviews with Dr. Kay. They were grown men from all walks of life. They were short and stout. They were tall and lanky. They were balding and missing teeth. They had gone to war in 'Nam. They had been in gunfights with bullets still lodged somewhere in their bodies. One or two had deformities, like a missing leg or arm, a missing eye, or a tube protruding from the neck to breathe. And, she had to admit, some were more attractive than others. So many different men, different ages and nationalities. Some aspiring, others burned out on life.

Kay had to say it over and over again for her ears only: "Only at Fort Dix."

Overall, these men became little boys before her, easily giving in, submitting to Kay as if she were a surrogate mother. Sure, they cried and cried, and they told all of their wild stories before her. But she was underwhelmed in most cases, sometimes even seeing right through the acts they performed before her. In other cases, she merely displayed her humility. How could she *not* have compassion for the convict whose father raped him continuously as a child? Or the one who was once a police officer whose life changed the day a burglar killed his entire family? How could she *not* feel for the convict who had undergone extreme torture having worked as an underling in Escobar's Colombian drug empire, with his severed foot as evidence to the horrors of that life? Day after day these experiences seeped into her consciousness, to the point where she thought she'd heard it all. But Jamel Ross was somehow different.

Driving home to her town house in Brownsville, New Jersey, just fifteen minutes away from the prison, less than that from the McGuire Air Force Base, Kay revisited her interview with Convict Ross. It was her rule to leave her caseload (and the thoughts that went with them) back on the prison compound. Don't take the job home with you, she always told herself. But this Ross fella, something about him made her quiver inside. She was having those intriguing notions again. Here was a man who she could say she'd never met before; nothing common or usual about him. And it wasn't any of the fame and excitement of the life he unveiled to her, either. It was *him*. Jamel Ross. He was of average looks; not the absolute *Ebony* man, but like an established actor, complete with his own special brand of peculiarities and, no doubt, fetishes. Two women, he'd said? Kay caught that mention and made an effort not to be affected either way. But that was then. Now she found *herself* stuck on stupid as she paid for a quart of orange juice at the local Wawa, a convenience store in town.

"Miss? You okay?" the clerk asked. The teenager gave her a funny look, holding the dollar that Kay had given her.

"Huh? Oh. I'm sorry, I was thinking it was a pint," Kay lied and took another dollar out to cover the full cost of the juice. It was bagged and Kay swiped it up to make her escape. "That lady is in Never-Never Land," Kay overheard the clerk commenting to the next customer. "Sure is," was the response.

Kay wouldn't be seeing Convict Ross for another two weeks for sure, unless she somehow passed him walking along the compound amidst other convicts in their movement to the chow hall, the gymnasium, or just making rounds as they did from day to day. Already she'd met with this convict a number of times—three times, as far as she could recall. But now she decided to go further into his background, when only under special circumstances did she have to pull a convict's file. Generally she didn't mix a person's background with her own professional opinion. She didn't want what she could learn on her own to be tainted by what other so-called professionals determined about the men to whom she had to listen. Jamel Ross, on the other hand, gave her reason enough to dig. Intrigue.

"You can take it down to your office if you want to, Kay. Just get it back to me as soon as you can," Nancy had said to Kay when she went to Records to see the convict's file.

"Oh? Thanks, Nance. That's helpful. This way I don't have to rush through the file. I owe you."

"No prob. Really, Kay. Let's do lunch sometime."

"Yeah. Let's," Kay replied.

Kay had gone to the housing unit where Ross

was assigned. There were seven units on Fort Dix that were situated in such a way so as to be at a good distance from one another. Although the institution wasn't built for this purpose, it had been just like the rest of the army base—an installation with the necessary facilities to accommodate battalions of men. Back in the day, these same buildings housed troops destined for Vietnam. To say the least, these same buildings, though well kept, were as old as Methuselah, and not exactly the best communal living has to offer. Brick, cinder block, plumbing, floor tiles, and semigloss paint. Nothing to it.

Jamel was among three hundred and fifty convicts living in Building 5852. Despite the overcrowded dorms, prisoners had no choice but to police themselves. More specifically, these men had to *behave* themselves during their prison stay, however brief or long. Certain privileges were instituted to ease the pain and suffering at Dix, including the use of pay phones, a half dozen televisions, a pool table, and three microwave ovens to heat commissary items. Each convict also maintained his own area (recognized as the "area of operation"), which included a locker for personal belongings and a bunk bed, whether upper or lower. However, no matter the conveniences, there was no substitute for freedom, at least not for *some* prisoners. Others had adapted to the life and kept returning time and again, as if this were their true comfort zone, the only one they cared to be a part of. Here, you could limit your responsibilities, you could get away from all the cares of the world you left behind, and you didn't have to worry about the expenses of food, medical care, or housing.

Kay was made well aware of the convicts' living conditions in her training for the position, and besides, she had to sit through hundreds of sessions with convicts who sniveled about this impropriety and that, about feeling shut in and confined, and above all, how they came to have problems surviving within a room of eleven men, each with his own individual package of cultural issues, religious beliefs, squabbles, rituals, and idiosyncrasies. During sessions she often secretly told herself, Buddy, if you can't do the time, don't do the crime. But she didn't dare act so cross toward the convicts. She merely listened and helped those men draw their own conclusions. She had to direct them so that they could come forth with their own answers to their own unique circumstances. Otherwise, there was nothing more that she could do for them. If they cried the blues, she couldn't call the judge and ask him to reconsider. If they had financial woes back home and their families were falling apart, she couldn't get them a furlough to help strengthen family ties. And no, she wouldn't fall for the ol' "I need a two-man room" trick, "or else I'll kill myself." Any mention of suicide would have to be immediately reported and the convict would be escorted to the special housing unit (called "SHU"), where he'd spend his days and nights in underwear and a T-shirt and the lights would remain on all the while. Kay could recall just one convict who required preferred housing, and it was only because he'd jumped out of a window at some point during his years of incarceration. Give 'im a room and keep 'im calm, she'd decided.

But as far as Convict Ross went, Kay saw that he had adapted well to his circumstances. Moreover, he was being productive during his sentence, reading and planning (*what*, she didn't know), where many others didn't have a clue as to how to handle this special brand of misery: incarceration.

Nancy's permission allowed Kay to take the Ross file to her office. But she also went beyond that and made a photocopy of certain documents before she returned the file to the unit office. Back home in her town house, about to chow down on the chicken and broccoli she had bought from the local Chinese restaurant, Kay pulled those same papers from her leather organizer.

It was just past six in the evening now and the major stories were being reported on NBC–10, but Kay was so busy burying her fork in the food and reviewing the paperwork that the world's concerns hardly mattered.

Pre-sentence Report: Jamel J. Ross (Aliases: "Jamel," "Slim," "Jay," "JR")

Convict Number: 40949–054

Sentence Date: 10/13/97

Offense: *Count One*: Conspiracy to commit bank fraud—18 U.S.C. §371 [1344 (1)]—five years/$250,000, a class-D felony.

Count Two: Bank fraud—18 U.S.C. §1344 (1) and (2)—30 years/$1,000,000, a class-B felony.

Arrest Date: 3/26/96

Release Status: Held without bail on March 27th, 1996

Detainers: None

Co-Defendants: Ruben Santano and Joe
  Weathers

Date Report Prepared: 06/05/97

IDENTIFYING DATA:

Date of Birth: 01/20/65

Age: 32

Race: Black, non-Hispanic

Sex: Male

Before Kay read further, she did the math in her head and determined that Jamel was thirty-six years old. And then she wondered about something else before picking up the phone and dialing.

"Dad? Hi. *Dad?!* It's me, *Kay*! I do *not* sound like Patrice; first of all, *she's* younger. So, if anything, *she* sounds like *me*. But you know darn well that Patrice has that Southern belle thing goin' on, ever since she moved south . . . okay then. Stop playin' me. See? I *knew* you knew, Dad. Always kiddin' around. I miss you, too. Well, yeah . . . I have a couple of questions for you. Law stuff . . . no, I don't think you have to pull out the law books to answer, but . . . okay. I'm lookin' at something called a PSI . . . right. It says here, under offense, count one is conspiracy to commit bank fraud. There's a reference number . . . right. How'd you know that?" Kay was making an effort to handle the papers, to cradle the telephone on her shoulder, and to eat, all at once.

"Do you mind if I put you on the speaker, Dad?"

Kay didn't even wait for an answer before setting the phone on its bed and pressing the speaker button on its console.

"You know how I hate that, darling."

"I'm just eating dinner, Dad, trying to do the most productive thing at every given moment . . . isn't that what you taught me?"

"I guess. What're you eating?"

"Chinese."

"I also taught you to make time in your schedule so that you wouldn't be stopping at every Tom, Dick, and Harry's fast food for a bite to eat. When are you gonna eat a real meal? That's the only way that you are going to keep fit, darling."

"Why don't you just say it, Dad? I'm fat."

There was a silence. Kay had a love/hate admiration for her father, the retired federal judge who knew her like a book. It was as if he could see through the phone.

"*Any*way, Dad, just so you know, I made breakfast and dinner for the last week straight. I'm just treating myself tonight. Got caught in traffic. You know the story. And . . . I just signed up at Bally's gym for a two-year membership."

"Excellent, no argument from me, doll."

"Okay. Now, could you take off the dad hat and put on the judge's robe for a moment?"

"Is this regarding a convict at the prison?"

"Mmm-hmm," Kay replied with a juicy stalk of broccoli wedged in her mouth.

"Okay, so you've got his PSI. What do you need to know?"

"On these charges, the conspiracy says five years and a quarter-million-dollar fine, and the bank fraud says thirty years and a one-million-dollar fine."

"Okay," her father agreed.

"But at Fort Dix, the computer says his sentence was eighty-four months with a release date of 2003. And there's less than a ten-thousand-dollar fine. How's that?"

"Well, the five years and the thirty years are the maximums that the offenses can warrant. But very rarely does a defendant get those numbers. There's something called sentencing guidelines set up by a commission. Reagan's work. It's supposed to control what we do on the bench because some judges abuse the bench, take payoffs, et cetera . . ."

"Did *you* ever take a payoff, Dad?"

"The one defendant who *did* offer is still doing time in Kansas. Folks'll be able to read telephone messages in thin air before he gets out of prison. Does that answer your question?"

"I hate to hear you talk like that, Dad. Some of these guys are human beings, you know."

"I guess. What else did you need to ask Judge Edmondson?"

"Well . . . here it says, under 'status of co-defendants,' they both entered a plea of guilty, but received no prison time. Both got supervised release."

"Standard for informants," said the judge. "They both had to cooperate and testify against him and the prosecutor leveraged for them to get off scot-free. Happens all the time."

"So they bought their freedom with their testimonies."

"Basically."

"Shady," said Kay.

"Again . . . happens all the time. But one of these days, the dam is gonna break."

"I can imagine. Just about every convict I've met had informants."

"But honey pie, the good guys have to have *something* to work with, otherwise everyone would get away with *everything*. We may as well change the name and the ethics of the nation to those of Sodom and Gomorrah, corruption and wickedness all over the place."

"Maybe so. I don't know what to think anymore. It's just so much . . . maybe too much to know both sides of the coin. On one end there's tradition, my upbringing, my respect for the law and democracy . . . also my training and my job. But on the other end, I look inside of these men's heads every day. I see and understand how they act. I know what makes them tick. Sometimes . . ." Kay faded off as though lost in thought.

"What, sugar?"

"Sometimes my compassion surfaces. I'm human."

"You certainly are. Which brings me to this . . . take a vacation for yourself, darling. Go down to North Carolina and visit your sister. Or maybe you should go and visit your auntie in San Diego. Just pull out for a bit to reevaluate life. We all need that once in a while, but rarely do we realize the importance of breathing room."

"Could be right, Dad. One other thing. This report talks about the convict as the head man, how he recruited others, 'conspired this' and 'provided that.' There's just too much here . . . as if this guy is, or was, the most notorious villain the government ever captured. Is this the way things really happened? I mean, is it all fact?"

The ex-judge chuckled and said, "Remember something else I always taught you, doll: Don't believe anything you hear and only half of what you see. Those PSIs are never one-hundred-percent correct. And more importantly, they're put together by people. The whole machine, with its wheels and gears and engines, depends upon people in order to operate. It's almost like a Ponzi scheme . . . you know, when the con is to attract and then confuse investors in order to pay off past investors. The cycle just never stops without fresh blood."

"That's interesting how you put it, the justice system, as a con."

"One day I'll sit down with you and explain how in many cases it *is* a con."

"Well, thanks, Dad."

"So can I look forward to a visit soon? Or am I to be left to die off like some dried-up tree bark . . . a dying oak."

"Don't say that, Dad. You know I love you the world over. I'll visit next week. Promise."

CHAPTER 3

Unit 5852 was a three-story building, like all the others at Fort Dix, with most of those tension-relieving activities working themselves out on the first floor, where the officers' station was situated. Various TV rooms branched off of the main hallway, the major passage through which convicts walked from one end of the building to the other. On the west side of that hallway there were four phones, individually sectioned off, allowing for greater privacy. So it never failed that there was a longer line of convicts on the west side who preferred waiting so that they'd have that added privacy. At the moment, Jamel was on the east side of the building, waiting outside the phone room where just four of the phones were housed. In this room, everyone could more or less hear everyone else's conversation. But Jamel didn't mind if this particular conversation was overheard since this wasn't going to be one of *those* calls that might inspire an embarrassing erection. His was just a call for money; nothing more, nothing less.

Gliss stepped up. "Who's last?"

"You," Roy answered.

"How come you always gotta say somethin' slick out cho' mouth, Roy? How 'bout if I just step to you and serve yo' ass. Would you like that shit?"

"Tell you what. I'll even close my eyes and you take your best shot," Roy answered.

As the bystander to this argument, Jamel started laughing, the hardest laugh he'd had in a while.

"Oh. So you think that shit's funny, too, huh?" Gliss was addressing Jamel and it provoked Jamel to laugh even more, holding his stomach now.

Gliss just stood there with a dumb look on his face, unappreciative of the disrespect. "Okay, okay . . . come on . . . who's last?"

"Me, nigga, what?" Roy wasn't smiling now.

"Aight, Roy. Chill. *Dag.* Why life gotta be so complicated?"

"Oh God." Jamel sighed, coming out of his bout

of utter elation. It was obvious to Jamel, as to anyone, that Gliss was two sizes smaller (in body and mind) than Roy and that any challenge or threat of bodily harm was indeed laughable. Suicidal even.

"Yo . . . did you hear they 'bout to sell CD players in the commissary?"

"Really?" Jamel said. But then Roy quickly jumped in to say, "Don't listen to him, Mel. That ma'fucka be lyin' his ass off sometimes."

"Dag, Roy! Can't *I* start a little rumor sometimes?"

"But that's what you *been* doin'. The last shit you made up was about the Supreme Court cutting the sentencing guidelines in half, got niggas all hot and excited in here."

"Oh damn. My bad. I thought . . ."

"You thought? Dude, niggas got thirty years and some mo' shit up in here. Let a thorough ma'fucka catch yo' ass with that bullshit."

"Split his wig back to the white meat," Jamel said.

"See . . . y'all ain't gonna be jumpin' all over me . . . I'm goin' down the way to use the phone where ma'fuckas ain't hatin' on a nigga." And Gliss stepped off with his funny ass.

"Something's wrong with that brotha," Jamel said.

"A few tools missin' from his shed," Roy added.

"But I *did* hear that the CD players they were supposed to buy for the rec department was shut down."

"Word?"

"After they did a shakedown up in rec and found all that contraband in niggas' lockers, they just changed up the priorities, I guess."

"Damn," Jamel said after sucking his teeth. "I'm hot about that too. I was lookin' forward to hearing all the new shit . . . damn."

"You? I'm on that Alicia Keys chick *hard*."

The two did a low-five hand slap in agreement.

"Every time I see her video, I choke up 'n' shit, like I *know* that bitch."

"You better not know her *too* good. And stop calling my wife a bitch."

"Your wife? Shit . . . then I had your wife up in the bed with me last night."

The two began to slap box playfully until it was Roy's turn to use the phone.

Irving was one of the four or five Hasidic Jews in the unit. He was next to use the phone and wagged his head in disgust at the mild roughhousing before him. Jamel saw into his attitude and ignored it.

Now Box stepped up. Jamel instantly gave him a pound. "'Sup, dog?"

"You last?" asked Box.

Jamel nodded. Box and Mel were bidding together for a year or so now, ever since Box was transferred from Fairton, the closest federal prison in the region. The two worked out together, ate together, and shared joys and pains.

"Box . . . *man*! I just met with the doc this morning."

"The female in Psychology?"

"Mmmm-hmmm."

"Fine *mothafucka*."

"Yeah, but come on, dog. You know dudes like us wouldn't give her a second look in the street."

"You're right."

"All a sudden, we locked up and plain ol' crackers start to look like a goddamn lavish banquet."

"True that."

"But check it. Man, I was spinning that bitch this mornin'. Had her head twisted."

"*Really!* Tell me—tell me. What happened?"

"I was spillin' shit about my crimes 'n' shit . . . you know, gettin' real personal. I even told her about JoJo and Deadra."

"Your baby mommas?"

"Yup. And she tried to play like that didn't touch her. But I could see right through her. I *know* that shit touched her. She had to be askin' herself, 'This guy had two lovers?'"

Box was visibly excited about the accounts.

Jamel continued, "So check it. She goes on about how I'm stupid for throwin' all that away."

"Say word?"

"Yup! Came right out of her face with that shit, and I went the fuck off on her. I played real *emotional,* like that shit *really* hurt my feelings. But inside, I was sayin', Lemme put this bitch in her place."

"What happened? Whadyou say?"

"I said, 'Who you think you are, talkin' to me like that? I'm locked up, oppressed, undignified . . .' all that. 'No sex. No women.' I let it all out. She said that she was trying to keep it real. But I didn't go for that. I put on the tears and everything. *Maaan!* That woman was trembling like I don't know what. I had her *shook*. She apologized and the whole nine."

"Then what?"

"Yo, she made the biggest mistake, dude. She got up and sat next to me on the couch and put her hand on my thigh. I almost came on myself."

"Get the fuck . . ."

"I had to hunch over just to hide my dick. I was as hard as a totem pole."

Jamel and Box slapped hands again, once, twice, then three times hard in acknowledgment of the milestone.

"Yo . . . while I was hunched over, my head in my palms, you wouldn't believe this bitch petted my head like a fuckin' Labrador or some shit."

Box was freaking out about the events, bangin' the wall with the side of his fists and stompin' his feet. Other prisoners took note of the excitement, obviously interested in all that was going on.

"So whatcha gonna do? You think she'll let you hit it?"

"I don't know. I mean, don't get me wrong . . . I wouldn't mind it. It's been a goddamn four-year stretch so far with no pussy. Right about now I'd take a one-eyed Norwegian amputee with alopecia." The comment drew heavy laughter.

"Dig it. Well, good luck, dog. Lemme know when it goes down. I'd pay mad mackerels and postage stamps to see that shit."

CHAPTER 4

Kay didn't tell Jamel what she'd learned about him, mainly because she didn't want him to feel intimidated. Already she felt she'd stepped over the line with the whole "stupid" comment. She didn't mean to hit him that hard—it just happened. She spoke from her heart, not from her professional opinion. So she'd imagined what a fierce blow it'd be to bring up his past: the informants, the various aliases he'd used in his bank scams, his Harlem connections, his mischief in high school, his parents' divorce, his withered financial status, or that a competency evaluation revealed a narcissistic personality disorder. She wouldn't dare bring up the report's essential feature: he had a grandiose sense of self-importance or uniqueness and he was preoccupied with fantasies of unlimited success. Kay chose to see Jamel as arrogant, not necessarily lacking in self-esteem, but yes, it was possible that he had that exhibitionistic need for constant attention and admiration, hence the two lovers back home.

And that was another thing that was making her more and more curious: *the women.* Jamel wasn't a shoo-in for a Chippendale's model, and he wasn't Denzel. He had that tall, dark, and handsome look of a basketball player, just not as tall. His PSI said five feet ten and 160 pounds. It said that he was in good physical condition with no tattoos or scars. Kay also called Allison over in Medical. Yes, Jamel was AIDS-free. But *why,* she asked herself after the call, did I need to know that? What bearing did such information have?

— — — —

"What are your feelings about success?" she asked Jamel at their next meeting.

"I try to keep a consistent focus on the things I want . . . on the goals I want to achieve. Success to me is a massive contribution to humanity. Like Thomas Edison made. Every time we cut on the lights, his legacy persists. I want to make a contribution of *those*

proportions. I want a big family and plenty of money—
sure. But most of all, I want to do something other
than the usual, something more than to merely exist.
In a thousand years, I want someone to know me, to
feel me and my presence. I don't care if it's a stranger
or a great-grandchild to the tenth power. I want them
to feel my power to the point where it guides their
life . . . where it opens doors to show them a better
way of life. An extraordinary way of life."

"That's a mouthful, Jamel."

"And it's a lot of work, too. Work I *know* I can do.
Work I *will* do."

Kay was thinking to herself, Yup, unlimited success
all right. But at the same time Kay believed what Jamel
believed. She was convinced that he would somehow
achieve what he wanted.

"Not by any means necessary, I hope."

"No. I can do what I need to do legit, if that's what
you mean. I won't be back here. *Ever*."

"That's good to hear. You know I've heard *that* before. Over and over again, as a matter of fact."

"But you know, this time was real valuable to me.
It meant sacrifice. It means that my sons, my nephews,
and my sons' sons will never have to go through this

just because I did. Now it's on me to make impressions on them."

Kay was silent. Stuck in the moment. The truth always commanded its own space in time.

"Sounds like you've got things all mapped out. So tell me, and keep it real . . . why do you still need *me*? Why the interview?"

Jamel took a moment to breathe and looked out the office window. "I'll tell ya, Dr. Kay . . . the world's greatest leaders need consultants. The president has his cabinet and his presidential advisors. Sherlock had Watson. Every superhero from Superwoman to the Fantastic Four had mentors or elders they looked up to for advice. And I believe that's always been my problem. I've always worked at life alone. But I'm convinced, especially now, that I've got to keep advisors in my ear. I must maintain dialogue with those outside of my world. And can I keep it real, as you say?"

"Please." Dr. Kay sensed that what Jamel had to say might be a little personal, but she was open to anything right now.

Was she opening up to him? Was this that moment in time that would change their "gatekeeper/prisoner" relationship to something more personal?

"It doesn't hurt that you're a black woman, either," Jamel finally said. He wanted to say *attractive* black woman, but his conscience didn't feel it was the right time. In his mind he kicked himself for not saying what he meant.

"How does that help you?"

"Well, for one, even though you're one of *them*," Jamel made the quote sign with both sets of fingers, "you're really a lot like *me* . . . set aside the plumbing."

"The plumbing?"

Jamel made with the gestures. "You know plumb-*ing*, as in a female's body. I'm comfortable with you, Dr. Kay."

"Oh. That's nice of you to say, Jamel." Kay's phone rang. "Excuse me, please." When she got up, Jamel began flipping through the book *Black Firsts* again.

"Can you excuse me?" Kay hinted that the conversation was more personal by her expression and Jamel removed himself. Out in the carpeted hallway, he peeked in now and again. It was only now that he wondered if she was married. There was no ring on her finger. And it didn't say *Mrs.* Dr. Edmondson on her door.

"Listen, Joe. I'm with a convict right now. This isn't

the time for chitchat." Kay made slight adjustments to the papers on her desk, forcing herself to feel too busy for her co-worker's phone call. Joe was a correctional officer at Fort Dix. He *was* tall like a basketball player with a very dark complexion, and he worked in the laundry this quarter. Next quarter he might be assigned to the commissary or even food service since COs were always at the mercy of the administrators. Wherever they were assigned, it was generally for five days a week, and their job was to make sure the prisoners followed their version of BOP policy. Meanwhile, everyone stayed alert and on the same page by two-way radio. It was a whole big maze that basically amounted to a routine of checks and balances.

"Lunch might work next week, Joe, but this week is really busy. Can I get back to you?"

When the call ended, Kay had to take her own deep breath, feeling as though she was juggling serious concerns, all of them pulling at her attention span. Her father, her caseload, the job, and now Joe. Wow, she thought to herself. One lunch with this guy and suddenly I'm burdened.

"Sorry, Jamel, where were we?"

"Success. Advisors. Plumbing."

"Right, right. You were in the process of telling me why you still need to see me."

"Well, besides advice, I've never had a therapist to guide me, ya know? Sometimes even I wonder if my head is right concerning how I am thinking and what I'm thinking about. I kind of look at this whole prison thing as my own growing-up process. And you're part of my healing. My lifesaver."

"What kinds of things do you think require healing?"

"For one, there's my personal life. I can tell if my direction is right. It feels right to *me*. But in the over-all scheme of things, I've been so concerned about my future and how this life is gonna play itself out. It's frightening sometimes. Does what I want jibe with nature?"

"You mean the kinds of success you want?"

"That. My lifestyle. My beefs."

"Whoa . . . slow down. What's so questionable about your lifestyle?"

"I do a lot of measuring these days; like back at the unit, I have eleven others in my room. So once in a blue moon I tend to weigh myself against the vultures and the hummingbirds."

Kay laughed. "The vultures? The hummingbirds?"

"Yeah, it's this African belief—and it's true, really—that in the desert, the vultures hunt and prey on the carcasses and that's all they do. It's how they survive. Dead carcasses."

"And the hummingbirds?"

"They're carefree. Unconcerned about the big, bad vultures. They're collecting honey all day, nectar from the flowers. Almost like stopping to smell the roses in life. But never do the vultures go after the hummingbirds and the hummingbirds are not affected by the vultures."

"If you don't mind me asking, Jamel, which are you?"

"Both, really."

Kay's face held a curious twist.

"Really. For the most part, I'm a hummingbird. I stay out of harm's way. I ignore the vultures with all their rah-rah talk and their rah-rah ways. They tend to be all the same. Tend to do all the same things. They love to talk; especially about themselves, what *they* have. What they did way back when. They impose themselves on whoever cares and if you don't care, they notice real quick. They take offense to it when you're not one of their followers."

"Interesting. I've never heard it put quite that way. So *you're* also like that sometimes?"

"I don't think I'm physically imposing. I only weigh a buck sixty and, no, I've never killed anyone before. But a vulture's mind . . ."

"The mind you once had when you were younger?"

"Exactly. That's something I revisit from time to time, where I'll wish harm on another, because I think he deserves it. Or I'll hate—not in terms of jealousy, never that, but just not keeping with my whole philosophy of doing time. That 'live and let live' attitude. *So what* if you sit in the mirror every day for hours pulling at your facial hairs—it's all good. *So what* if you brush your hair for three hours a day—it's all good. Do *you*."

"They do that?"

"*Do* they? Doc, if I told you the things I see every day, you'd freak. Yeah, the guy that pulls at his hairs is real. He uses tweezers and it's an everyday thing. A hair here, a hair there. It can be very annoying if you let it. But when I'm in my right mind I keep that compassion about me. I figure, let the guy live; he probably has serious mental problems. And there's probably still a trace of drugs left in his system. Insecurities, peculiarities; there's a whole lot of reasons for our actions, no doubt. But because I'm forced to live in the same room, I've gotta stay focused and let him be. I've gotta let go of the hate. I gotta have compassion."

"So you want compassion to be a part of your lifestyle."

"You got it. Compassion. Humility. Consideration and a wee bit less arrogance. I want to stay human and likeable. With an open face. You know—*approachable*."

"*Wow* . . . you really *do* know what you want. Okay, so then what about the other issues you talk about? Your beefs?"

Jamel wagged his head. "I don't know if there's enough time in the day for that, Doc. It's so much."

"We've got another twenty minutes together. If you start to bore me, I'll let you know. Unless it hurts to unveil your feelings, I . . ."

"See, you got jokes."

"Well, you *did* go to the tears last time. And I feel like I'm walking on eggshells with you now."

"Funny. I kind of feel that way, too."

"How so?"

"You a doctor first, or a cop?"

"What?"

"Are you a doctor first . . . or a cop? You're obviously trained to deal with convicts. If a riot goes down in here, you know you gotta act accordingly."

"Jamel, this is a paycheck for me. At the end of the day I'm a black woman trying to make a living. Trying to make a difference."

"But you didn't answer me."

"I'm . . . I'm a human being, Jamel. And, if possible, I'd appreciate it if you saw me as your friend."

Jamel said nothing for a time. Then he held a serious expression and said, "Well, Doc, I feel like I'm limited in what I can say; in what I *wanna* say. I wanna be open with you, but I also feel like there are all kinds of spiderwebs between us. If you say something out of line, you can hurt me. If I say something out of line, you can press the panic button. In both instances, *you're* the winner."

Jamel could actually see Dr. Kay taking a deep breath as she got up from her desk and approached the couch to sit beside him. Jamel was immediately concerned with the possibility of someone passing by, perhaps peeking into that narrow window in the door. And now her hand was on his thigh, the second time. Jesus Christ, he said silently.

"Jamel, let's stop the bullshit. You're thirty-six, I'm thirty-three. You went into black entertainment, an entrepreneur; me, I went to school for six years to be a psychotherapist. Now here we are, governed by the very same folks at the BOP. They pay me and tell me what to do. They hold the keys and tell you when to go home. But be clear, Jamel; there are no microphones in here and I'm not recording anything. What you say here to me, in this office, is between *you*"— Dr. Kay fingered Jamel's chest, and then her own as she said—"and *me*. Capeesh?"

"Capeesh," Jamel replied. Except right here and now he felt like his bowels were about to give, considering the emotions letting loose in his body. Now, encouraged to speak, Jamel did have a few questions to try on her.

"So, you married?"

"No. Engaged once."

"Did you live in with him?"

After a chuckle, Dr. Kay asked, "Why is that always an *issue* with men? You always wanna know if the land has been farmed."

Jamel smiled at her deep understanding and said, "Well, has it been?"

And now, Dr. Kay was smiling, too. Plus, Jamel could see her tongue playing along the inside of her cheek. She had no idea what that was doing to him.

"Well, if you wanna know, the land has indeed been farmed. And farmed *well*, I might add. I had a man friend for quite a few years; he taught me everything he knew." Dr. Kay stood up and smoothed her hands along her sides as if to outline all of her package. Then she finished by saying, "And the rest I picked up on my own."

A big *wow* glowed in Jamel's mind.

"Okay. Now you want the truth?" Jamel said nothing before Dr. Kay said, "My father would kill me if he heard about me shacking up with a man and not getting married."

"Daddy's little girl, huh?"

"To a degree. He advises me, but I have my own opinions and I make my own decisions. I'm a big girl, if you haven't noticed."

"You sure are," Jamel felt bold enough to say. Then, in a lowered tone, he said, "So, can I ask . . . are you sure your office isn't bugged? Like, maybe the man is tryin' to listen in to our minds without you knowin'?"

"Negative. My daddy was the first to ask me about that. Then I had a CO I know in to check it out."

Jamel guessed who that might be.

"Hmmm, so I can say what I want? I can say whatever's on my mind?"

"Within reason," she said with leery eyes.

"Okay. Here goes. I'm feelin' you. Your image, your intelligence, your poise. Your down-to-earth demeanor."

"Thank you. That's sweet of you. You're incredibly witty, bright, and I do like that arrogance about you. It's subtle, yet effective. Mysterious, even."

"Doc, there's something else."

"Oh boy. Let 'er rip." Her eyes were fixed now, practically daring Jamel. Except he took it as a warning. I'd better not, he told himself. And he wagged his head.

"No, go'won."

"Nah. Maybe on our next meeting."

Dr. Kay took another deep breath. "Okay, then. Your call. So, you wanna tell me about those beefs? Are we talking about *in here*? Or at home?"

"At home. There's a cop in my neighborhood who hunted me."

"No shit."

"Straight up. We went to the same schools. Pursued some of the same homegirls. He was the jock. I was the knucklehead. You get the picture.

"Of course. But while he was bangin' hood rats at an early age, I was getting busy with my big dreams. Just like my father did, back in Yonkers. I mean, Dad was only doin' floors 'n' stuff, but he grew it into a big business. Then I was doin' my thing; little handyman jobs here and there. I even made the local papers."

"I remember you showed me that."

"And that little talent show I used to have for the kids in the area. We need that type of stuff in our hood."

"So what happened?"

"I think it was me, the big fish in the small pond. I know some people got jealous. Others loved what I was doin'; appreciated how a young black man was makin' somethin' out of nothin'. But I had my haters, too. Like Officer Bo Simmons. Hay-*ter*."

"How so?"

"He arrested me for some bullshit traffic infractions. Once when I had a squabble with one of my girls at home, he was one of the officers who showed up." Before Dr. Kay could wonder how the police got into it, Jamel said, "Thanks to a nosy neighbor. But the argument was already squashed. Except Simmons made a bigger deal out of it, saying he had the authority to arrest me even if the woman didn't wanna press charges. He said I was 'intimidating' her."

"Did you?" she asked.

"No. The argument had long since ended. Nothin' but the usual boy-girl shit. Besides, the woman was dead wrong. She came out of her face and disrespected me. Women get crazy sometimes."

"Really? And men don't?"

"Now, I know you're not gonna sit there and deny that women are more emotional than men," he replied.

"No, I'm not. But I'm also not gonna sit here and ignore how men abuse women—physically and mentally."

"Whoa. Okay, I'm not goin' there today. Maybe that's a subject we can get into in the future. But as far as Bo Simmons goes? He was definitely aware of my street game, how I was doin' legal and illegal shit."

"So exactly how far did this hate go?" Dr. Kay was intrigued.

"Well, once I was at the local pizza shop waitin' for my order. There were a bunch of teenagers out there, too. But when Five-O rolled up—Bo being one of them—they asked everyone for ID. Like *he didn't know who I was.* Then he ordered all of us up against the wall, him and his sidekick, and they searched us. This motha—" Jamel was showing signs of rage, curling his lips and growling his words. "This *man* reaches under and grabs my testicles so hard it hurt for three days. I can still feel the pain in my mind to this day."

"Wow. He really *didn't* like you, huh?"

"I really didn't care if he did or didn't like me. I just wanted to be left alone. But he wanna keep finding shit to get at me. When he violated me like that, it was over."

"How so?"

"I'm goin' home in eighteen months or so, Dr. Kay, and I gotta face the same dumb shit. Plus, I'll be on probation. So can you imagine what I'm dealing with?"

"I can. What'll you do, Jamel?"

"For one, I'd like to free myself of that man while I'm trying to sleep at night."

"You mean, you have nightmares about him? Here?"

"Do I? I prob'ly shot that man in the head more times than Elmer Fudd shot at Bugs."

"Is that your only issue?"

"Not quite. I got one more enemy."

CHAPTER 5

If there are two sides to every story, then Jamel Ross and his growth in the community could be detailed in quite a few ways. But for sure, he had to be discreet about what he told and who, especially in prison. In here, there was that "crabs in a barrel" mentality, where people hungered to obtain available resources by any means necessary. However, when he *did* tell his stories, it went beyond "keeping it real." Jamel instead kept it *raw*. The watered-down version was for Dr. Kay Edmondson. But with Box, Twan, or any one of the eleven other roommates in his dorm, Jamel spit venom and passion and truth. And his "other enemy" as well as the "beef" he had with Mac Daddy was just that type of story. It was hot on his conscience, and kept him wide awake through many a sleepless night.

The 1990s set a tumultuous climate for black entertainment. For years, rhythm and blues had been penetrating the music charts. It was the Temps, Tops, and Supremes laying the groundwork in the 1960s; it was Isaac Hayes, Barry White, Donna Summer, and the Commodores who kept the mercury rising in the seventies; and it was Heatwave, Michael Jackson, Luther Vandross, and Whitney Houston who carried the torch well into the nineties. The LAPD beat Rodney King's ass for all the world to see and massive riots resulted when the cops were found not guilty. This event and others further fueled the "Fuck the Police" movements, where dozens of recordings were produced and marketed in response to the broad and blatant social inequities. Ice-T, NWA, Snoop Dogg. Eazy-E. Gangsta rap. Drive-by shootings, Crips and Bloods, and *Boyz n the Hood* were all images, titles, and themes that yielded constant pressure from masses of underprivileged people who lashed out at the nation's institutions of law and order. And while the West Coast spearheaded a movement all their own, the East Coast had its own spokespersons like

Public Enemy, X-Clan, and KRS-One, who maintained a conscious message in the air thanks to the various media platforms. Thanks to MTV, the revolution was *indeed* being televised.

Just like any other newborn, hip-hop struggled to become the multibillion-dollar industry it is today. Those few boutique labels that lobbied for sales and airplay made important beginnings that eventually earned recognition and energy for hip-hop. Inevitably, the formulas of hip-hop and R&B, hip-hop and pop, and even hip-hop and rock caused the genre to explode. This was what Jamel knew, things he had to explain in order to lay the foundation of his beef.

And now he was saying, "So, if you know the whole hip-hop story like they tell it on MTV, then you know who the godfather of the industry is."

"Russell Simmons," said Twan.

"Exactly. And under Russell was this rapper named Doctor Love."

"Oh, damn. That's goin' way back. Wasn't he down with Pumpkin and the Profile Allstars?"

Jamel reached out and gave Box a strong hand slap for hitting the nail right on the head.

"Bingo," said Jamel. "And if you know Doctor

Love's story, then you know who *he* brought into the business. His name is Mack, the one who started the whole Bulldog Records, with all those rappers and singers from the *New Jack City* era."

Twan nodded in response as Jamel put the puzzle together.

"He interned, he got to know people, and he eventually started his own label."

"I know, I know. I might be from the dirty-dirty, but I know my hip-hop science, Jay."

Jamel was amused at Twan's choice of words: "Hip-hop science."

"So, shit, you cut my story in half, Twan. So lemme bring you up to speed and how I play into the game."

Twan made a disbelieving face.

"See, when I was eighteen, I was already doin' business with Russ. His office wasn't but yay big; maybe half the size of this dorm room. I'm talkin' money changing hands, mad phone conversations, the whole nine." Jamel reached in his locker and pulled out his photo album.

Twan said, "I already seen your flicks, Jay."

"Nah, Twan. You ain't seen what I'm about to show you," said Jamel. And he slipped an envelope from between the cardboard back cover of the photo album.

"*Aww, damn!* Nigga got a secret compartment," Box hollered.

"Shhhh!" Jamel hissed. "The fuck, Box? You wanna put up a billboard or sumthin'? This is my stash spot for shit I don't want nosy COs to see." Jamel carefully kept some of the photos out of eyesight.

"Now, how you gonna do that, Jay? We supposed to be boys and you gonna hide the good shit?" Twan didn't miss what Jamel was trying to hide.

"Twan, a nigga's gotta have *somethin'* private. My girls is *my* girls at the end of the day. I ain't tryin' to have you or *nobody else* fantasizing about what's mine."

"Could you show us the picture already?" said Box.

Jamel pulled a picture of him and Russell, him and Doctor Love, then another with him and the Mack, all pictures taken at parties, according to the settings, the people, and lighting in the background.

"So, as I was sayin', I was doin' business with these dudes a long time ago. Russell, Love, and all a' them. Today niggas can't even get an audience with these cats. You can't even get on the *phone* with them; you gotta *be* somebody. *Feel me?*"

Twan was nodding his head now, speechless

"So back when Mack was just Mike, playin' ball at Yonkers High School, I was knee-deep in the game. I was livin' in the *belly* of hip-hop when it was bein' born."

"You went to school wit' 'em?"

Nodding, Jamel went on to say, "He was a freshman when I was a senior. But I didn't really recognize him like that back in the day. I only knew him as Mike Williams, until he started to play ball. He wasn't even that good, he just profiled good. The jock who got the girls."

"I know the type," said Twan.

"Lemme find out you were one of them, Twan."

"Mighta been, Jay. It's quite possible." Twan's eyes smiled, even if he didn't. Plus, the way he tried to answer the question, all intelligent-like, made the three guys laugh all at once.

"Well, Mike—I mean, Mack—took his court personality to the music industry, he promoted some parties; you know those old parties where they used to say 'special invited guests,' with all those celebrity names on them, tryin' to trick the average partygoer—well, the oldest trick in the book worked for him. Then, before you know it, one thing led to another and now the dude is a rapper."

"I ain't mad at 'em," said Twan.

"Me, *neither*," said Jamel. "I mean, good for him to get in where he could fit in. But just don't come up in here causin' trouble for the ma'fuckas who paid dues, too. Nah *mean*?"

"True, true." Jamel and his audience of two were sitting there in folding chairs at Twan's bed, while just two others were present in the room. Mr. Kale had his headphones on, the music loud enough to make sure the others in the room could hear *his* rendition of some song by the Mamas and the Papas. Meanwhile, White Boy Bob was up on his bunk at the other end of the room, close enough to hear, but heavily involved in a smut magazine. For the most part, this was as private as private could get at Fort Dix.

■ ■ ■ ■

Before his conviction, Jamel had a weekly ritual of visiting the nightclubs that were considered "hot spots" in and around New York City. This was his means of escape, since the daylight was when he carried out his spree of bank jobs. And everyone from the convicts in his midst, to the COs, to Dr. Kay wanted to know what happened. How had he fallen so hard, so fast? But

according to Jamel, it really wasn't the big deal everyone was making it out to be. There were bills, there
were loans that were due, and his little legit business
had gone belly-up. What else was there to explain?
He learned the scam of depositing phony checks and
withdrawing cash on them before they came due. *Period. End of story*. Nobody needed to know about the
guns. Nobody needed to know about his *other* street
activities. And, even if they'd asked, he wouldn't have
told them because "telling" anything really wasn't in
his heart. The check game was all he chose to expose
because the check game was over. The floating of
paper was old and antique, and high-tech computers
had put an end to it all.

"So it was check schemes by day and clubbin' by
night," Jamel explained to his roommates. "There was
the Peppermint Lounge in Jersey, Tipton's in Connecticut, but mostly we'd go to Manhattan, Harlem, or
Queens. There were hot spots in the city for almost
every night of the week. On Sunday, we'd do Chaz
& Wilson's on Seventy-ninth Street or the Uptown
Comedy Club in Harlem. Monday night was sports
night at Manhattan Proper in Queens, or we might
just drop in on Well's in Harlem for their chicken and

waffles." Jamel was rattling on about his various out-
ings and the women who he'd befriended in the meantime. "But, no matter what, even though we rolled
with four and five dudes, we never ran into trouble.
We weren't *lookin'* for any. Shit, there was money to
get the next morning. Anyway, getting back to Mack;
it was a warm Friday night in the summer of ninety-
six when me, Roscoe with One Eye, and my man Troy
stopped into PJ's, that spot up on One-thirty-second."

"Uptown," added Box.

"Right. And the nigga Roscoe had only been with
us for a minute, barely starting an internship with us.
But we brought him for the ride. And Troy's my man
who held me down when I had my little talent shows
back in YO. Anyway, the owner Pat is my homegirl
from YO too. So she introduces me to this dude who
says he's from Drop Dead Records and he's here tryin'
a set up Death Row East. And he passes us free T-
shirts—I guess as a gesture, or promotion, really. And,
not thinkin' of it, we threw 'em on just like that. They
had some quality to 'em and they said DROP DEAD
EAST in big bold letters. We were like *whatever.*"

"Okay," said Twan, assuming that this was all
harmless.

"'Let's get together and make somethin' happen,' the dude says. We said, 'Cool,' and that was the end of it. Me, Troy, and Roscoe had headed from PJ's to a club called Downtime in lower Manhattan. DJ Red Alert played there regularly and tonight was one of those nights. So, needless to say, there was a large amount of clubgoers outside, all of them waiting to get through the velvet rope, all of them looking to be accepted by the woman with the clipboard."

Jamel and Troy were too familiar with the nightlife and how things clicked. And since this was one of those impromptu visits, their names weren't likely to be on anyone's list. So Troy stepped to the bouncer at the club's exit and, after a few words, the three went in through the side door of Downtime.

"'This place reminds me of the old Danceteria,' I said at the time. 'A lot of floors, different music playing in different rooms. Plus the whole psychedelic look with the fluorescent art on the walls is dope. It looks more like a clubhouse than a nightclub.'

"'Where was Danceteria?' Roscoe had asked.

"'You're too young to know,' Troy had nearly shouted to be heard over the banging music that filled the club. Meanwhile, the three of us were weaving through the crowd of dancers, drinkers, and others who go to clubs to do neither. 'It's an old-school spot, like the Garage, the Limelight, and the Fun House. All of those spots are closed now.' We continued touring the club, making new discoveries, checking out the faces, and trying to hear each other speak up until we reached the DJ booth.

"'Yo, Red. Wassup!' I was the first to speak.

"'Peace, ya *bum*!' Troy stepped in to give Red a pound.

"'No, *you* a bum!'

"The back and forth name calling had Roscoe a little confused up until Troy had to whisper that 'bum' meant 'black unified male' in his ear. Then Red Alert turned his attention back to the turntables, mixed a new record in, and lowered his head to the microphone.

"'Big, big, big, *big*-big-big-big-big shout goes to my man Jay from Drop Dead Records. I got a free T-shirt up here for the first one who come up to the DJ booth. Compliments of Drop Dead, y'all!' It didn't matter that Red Alert got the information a little twisted; as long as he said *something*. It felt good just the same to get some acknowledgment from a famous DJ.

"Twan, we weren't even *thinkin'* of trouble when we left the club," Jamel continued. "I remember it was about one in the morning, but there was a mob scene outside. Everyone was trying to get in, but the capacity had reached its limit. Plus, there was a lot of racket in the street; loud music, some street marketing team, and people standing on their cars. Only thing on my mind was to get to the Jeep across the street so we could head back home." Jamel could feel himself reliving the moments that led up to the evening's drama, even though he was the only one to know how hot things were about to get.

"So, we reach the Jeep, start it up, and guess who pulls up beside me?"

"Mack."

"Exactly. And I thought he wanted my parking space or somethin', 'cause there was nowhere to park out there. So I pull out and I ease down the block. Next thing you know, that nigga's followin' me . . ."

"Okay, gentlemen. Shakedown! Shakedown! Shakedown!" Four corrections officers entered the dorm room with empty trash liners in their hands. As if there were a police emergency, one of them smacked the bunk a few times to wake White Boy

Bob, who had fallen off to sleep with the smut magazine in one hand and his crotch in the other. Mr. Kale didn't need a hint and was quick to get out of his bunk, into his slippers, and he stood with his hands up to be frisked.

"All right, you know the drill, fellas." Box and Twan grieved some, considering how Jamel's story was interrupted, but they also got up to stand, they got frisked, and then left the room so that the COs could perform their random search.

"Mothafuckas just wanna look in our personal pictures," said Box.

"Or Kale's feem books; you know that dude got the whole *Penthouse* library in his locker," said Jamel.

Twan made a face. "Well, Jay. That stuff tends to excite some folks." Twan injected some of his down South rationale while the three moved outside. They were eventually standing behind the five-foot fence that enclosed the Fort Dix softball field. A game happened to be in progress and it gave the guys something to look at as Jamel went back into the streets with his story.

"So where was I?"

"Mack."

"Right. So Mack was drivin' this platinum Mercedes coupe with some big husky security cat in the passenger's seat. You know he was ballin' by now, ever since his artist, Gonja, hit it big with his triple-platinum joint the year before. So I'm thinkin' the old beef we had was squashed, plus, that nigga was makin' mad dough by that time, so I couldn't see why he was interested in me."

"That nigga's shit was *nice,* too. That's the first album I'm getting when I get home," said Box, all off the subject. "But that otha joint—"

"*Anyway,*" said Jamel, trying to keep his story building and his memory intact, "Mack pulls up to the passenger side of the Jeep real slow-like. All of us had our windows down cuz it's hot as shit out. Plus, my air-condition wasn't kickin' correct. Dude pulls up to the rear window first. He goes 'wassup' to Roscoe. And Roscoe actually *answers* that mothafucka! Like they *buddies* 'n' shit. And that nigga knows I had beef with Mack. So it was like—"

"Homey was a traitor."

"Well, you ain't heard the half. After Roscoe answered and made that nigga feel all comfortable, Mack pulled up to the next window, where my man Troy was sittin'. He goes 'wassup' to Troy, and Troy just gives 'im a head nod. Cuz *that's my nigga*. In other words, any way that nigga wanna play it, Troy was still down wit' me, *feel me*? I mean, go'won and give respect, but at the end of the day, that's *my* nigga."

"So what happened next?" asked Twan, less interested in the double play that just went down on the softball field.

"Mack looks around Troy and says, 'Wassup, *bitch*.' But I straight ignored that nigga, cuz every week that nigga was in the newspapers about some kind of drama. And plus, I had been tryin' to be productive in life, *yah mean*? I coulda played it any way he wanted, but I chose to keep my cool. So instead of sayin' some *dumb* shit back, I just told that nigga, 'Listen, you keep your drama to y'self. I'ma mind my business, you mind yours.' If it wasn't for the red light, I wouldn't have no chance to answer this fool—but he goes, 'Nah, you a bitch.' Like he was sayin', 'Nah, I wanna start some shit tonight.' And that's when my boy Troy turned and looked at me like, 'whatcha gonna do?'"

Box licked his lips like he was ready to sink his teeth further into Jamel's story. Meanwhile, the cheering in the stands seemed to add to the escalation in the story; as if those convicts were aroused from actions that had happened years earlier. The batter went to second base and the man on second advanced to third.

"Eventually, I said, 'If I'ma bitch, pull over and show me I'ma bitch.' So you shoulda seen this fool; he looks at Husky in his passenger's seat, as if he needed approval, then he turns around and starts stutterin', 'A-aight.' And I know he ain't want no parts of me, cuz my man'll tell ya, I whupped dudes twice my size. I mean, I ain't sayin' I'm unbeatable, but the way I was feelin', I was ready to serve his ass right there in the middle of the street, platinum albums or no platinum albums."

Box was buggin' out, clutching the fence as if to pull the words out of Jamel's mouth. But if Jamel were to talk any faster, he'd choke on the air he took in between sentences.

"Did you ever think that Mack was hot at seein' you in them Drop Dead T-shirts? You know he got beef with them niggas on the West Coast. I heard they chased his ass out of town once, all the way to the airport."

"You know . . . I been down four years and change so far, Box. And I swear, I thought about *every angle* and *every scenario* tryin' to figure out why that all went down. It could've been the T-shirts, *yeah*. It coulda been he had a smoke before he saw me and it made him feel like Superman. And it could've been the stupid beef between us; but we even squashed that. It coulda been *anything*. The point is, Mack felt like makin' trouble that night, so eventually, I'm like, aight, me too."

— — — —

Adrenaline-driven, Jamel pulled over so abruptly that a wheel of the Jeep climbed onto a curb at an awkward angle in the well-lit section of Herald Square. It was just a few blocks from where the club was located, only without parked cars, crowds, or unwanted attention. Sure, this was the busiest part of the city by day, but at almost two in the morning, this was a very isolated New York City street that was about to see a fight go down.

What started out as heated words between Mack and Jamel quickly turned into something more. Jamel hit the ground running, ready to clear the air about who was the bitch. Mack emerged from his vehicle, as well, only he wasn't alone. Just when the two were about to clash, there were sounds of screeching tires. They were deafening sounds that tore into Jamel's sense of safety. At the same time there was a gunshot sound, then more tires screeching.

"Jay! It's an ambush! Go! Go! Go!" Troy's voice was loud enough, but his warning fell on deaf ears. Jamel never slowed. From the corner of his eye he saw the husky dude pull a weapon, except he wasn't threatened. He felt as though Mack's fame was powerful in one sense and his burden in another. Quick calculation told Jamel that he wouldn't be shot dead if the fight was fair, and so he continued on. Mack swung first. Jamel ducked, but just as quickly bounced back to an upright stance. And now Jamel threw a wild punch that caught Mack in the ear. There was an angry "mothafuck!" and then Mack charged at Jamel headfirst. Jamel was quick enough to get the party-promoter-turned-rapper into a headlock. But for Jamel, that's when things got rough. Someone grabbed him from behind and he found himself in an air-tight chokehold. A second later it was a cluster of bodies that inevitably weighed down on top of both Troy and Jamel until they were pushed to the pavement.

Jamel explained, "We were outnumbered by four or five others, as well as his big husky body-guard. I wondered where all the extra guys came from, but I later realized that Mack had an entourage following behind him. They came at us with bats and somebody pistol-whipped Troy. I felt fists and some-thin' else hard hit me in the cheek. That's why I got this scar under my eye. I think one of 'em had brass knuckles or somethin'."

"Bitch-ass nigga!" grunted Box.

Then Twan said, "No wonder he wanted to start somethin', cuz his wolves had his back the whole time. You went *in* a loser. Suicide."

"Right-right," Jamel said with the biggest smile he could manage. "But I came out alive. And that was his *biggest* mistake right there."

"And what happened to Roscoe? Where was he when it all went down?"

"Like you said, Twan. Traitor. And I shoulda smelled that from a mile away. I visited his little rented room one day to see how he was livin', and I seen a poster of Mack up on the wall. So I knew that bitch-ass was sweatin' him from jump."

"Dayum, Jamel. You caught some bad luck, for real. And the truth? Even though I don't know Mack like you did? Ever since I seen that boy all up on MTV, I didn't like him. And you know I get along with every-body, Jay. But somethin's so phony about that dude. All that thug shit he be sellin' on wax, man . . . lemme tell you, if he ever did me dirty, I'd bitch-slap that nigga. Point blank, Jay. And all them mothafuckas that roll with him? Them dudes ain't nothin' but hungry-ass niggas. They depend on that boy to make money so he can keep food in their mouths. They just like wolves; and the only way to tame wolves, I say, is with fire, Jay." Twan, the good-boy-turned-killer.

"But Jay, you know what kinda lawsuit you could bring against that nigga? He got mad melh now. He's known worldwide. You could get the biggest lawyer in the world to fight the case for you for nothin'. You need to think about that instead of some revenge."

Jamel turned to Box and put his hands on his shoulders. "Do you even realize what you're *saying*? You're telling me to run to the man and tell him, 'Mack and his boys jumped me.' Then when it comes to a trial, I'd have to get on somebody's witness stand and say, 'That man and his boys jumped me.' Box! *Look at me!* Do I look like that *next* hot mothafucka to you? That shit goes against everything I stand for. Word?" When Jamel took his hands off Box, the eyes said it all; the suggestion died right there where it was born. And there was no reason to say another word about it.

CHAPTER 6

"Now you really have me curious," Dr. Kay offered in a most compassionate tone. "They jumped you and left you there? Were there police? Were there witnesses? Did anybody—"

"No. No. And no," Jamel replied. "The last thing I remember seeing is somebody's foot coming down on my face. Next thing I know, I woke up in the hospital. I was able to use my brain, that's all I remember, and I was glad for that. Troy was on life support and nobody knew anything about Roscoe. I know the Jeep was impounded. But while they were going through the truck for evidence, they found a whole bunch of other stuff; the fake licenses and checks we used to use. All the paperwork on the banks we robbed."

"Woooooooow," exclaimed Dr. Kay. "You've really got a story to tell."

"Nah. This story can't be told, cuz it ain't over."

Dr. Kay seemed to want to overlook that comment and said, "So this is the stuff I read about or hear about on the news. I must've missed this story."

Jamel was wagging his head. "You wouldn't have heard any of this on the news, Doc, because I ain't a snitch. It happened, I survived, and he'll get his."

"Okay. I need to say this. You mind?"

"Go right ahead."

"You sound like a cliché."

Jamel twisted his face, unsure of what she meant.

"Okay. You're a convict, er . . . an ex-con—since you're all done with crimes, *right?* Well, all convicts hate police and want to get back at them."

"But—"

"Wait a minute. I'm not done. Then I've been counseling a lot of you guys now, enough to know that convicts—"

"Ex-cons."

"Right. *Ex*-cons have a *big* problem with rappers out there making money, building powerful fan bases, talking about or alluding to crimes they might've done and the criminal lifestyle when, obviously, they're not actually *doing* crime—they're rapping. Oh yeah; I know what the talk of the compound is, Jamel. There's a sort of complaint which is justified, I guess, to you all. I think you guys somehow look at them as liars. Am I *right* or wrong?"

"Yes. I guess that's right. They're rapping about what we do. And what we do is what sells their CDs and movies. Except *they're* the ones getting paid. We don't get jack. But really . . . there would be a *whole* lot of dead rappers if dudes really cared about that. In most cases you'll find that *real* gangstas and crooks hardly watch that stuff. They got more *important* issues, like taking somebody's head off. Trust me, Doc; I ain't no 'cliché hater,' or whatever you called it. I got certain issues with certain people. Nothing more, nothing less."

"I see." Dr. Kay took a deep breath and sighed. "Too much riffraff for me. But now I see what you mean by beef. I can see how you'd be bitter."

"Y-yeah. You could call it that. Just a *wee* bit bitter."

"So, that was it? You never went further with the issue?"

"Nope. This all happened just like that. All at once. I coulda died out there."

"So . . ." Dr. Kay sighed again. "Let's wrap up here for today. Tell me how you'd feel better about all of this street stuff. How do you think you'll be able to free yourself from the past? And what can I do to help you?"

"That's a mouthful, Doc. How can I feel better? If I could sleep at night and not twist and turn. That ambush really fucks with my head. Bo Simmons friskin' me with his grimy hands also fucks with my head."

"Do you dream about anything else? What do you dream about that's *good*? I mean, we've been sitting here for an hour and the most you've spoken about is what's hurting you. But what makes you feel good, Jamel?"

"You really wanna know?"

Dr. Kay nodded and shrugged at the same time.

"Sex. I'm like Adidas. All day I dream about sex." Jamel tried to conceal the smile behind his lips but didn't have much success. "I like to go back to the wild times with JoJo and Deadra. And there were a few before those two came around. Rain and I had a child together but, speaking of bitter, she took the child and disappeared when she found out I'd been with another woman. That was another girl; this dancer I met named Janine." Jamel's eyes widened at the thought, a gesture that said more than words could about those past experiences. "But my best memories are of JoJo and Deadra. Having two women who love you to the bone is a great experience."

"Mmm-hmm . . ." Kay murmured as if to scold Jamel for his sins.

"And thoughts that would make me feel free?" Jamel, with a deep breath, continued, "I'm hopin' that the freedom issue is resolved in the next eighteen months."

"Sort of freeing your body and mind at the same time? You know those are two different issues, right?"

"I guess."

"I'd like to help you free your mind, Jamel. Let's focus on some options and talk about that next time we get together."

- - - -

That evening, Kay was back to her old quickie routine again. At one point she thought of renting a movie, maybe a human-interest story to take her away from all of those crazy prison issues. Maybe something with Angela Bassett, or something deep with Morgan Freeman. Something with a feel-good message in it. But while Kay ate her chicken and broccoli dinner (the kind of fast food that never let her down), she was stuck on BET for a time. *106 & Park* was on and that pretty-ass host named Free had another pair of her fly-ass boots on, teasing and daring her sidekick about possibly wearing his hair out in an Afro (along with her) for a future show. Eventually they introduced their guest for the day.

"So, without further ado, give it up for the one and only *Mack*!"

Kay turned up the volume with her remote, but in her hurry to do so spilled a piece of that warm, gooey chicken down the front of her shirt. She yelped at how icky it felt, and she cursed herself for being so clumsy as she rose up from the couch to go clean up. Two videos and ten commercials later, Kay was back in front of the TV, feeling naked, her blouse and brassiere left in the bathroom hamper. She settled for a little wipe here and there for the time being. No sense in doing any major washing since she'd be in the shower soon. In the meantime, she was feeling a little naughty, all exposed like she was in front of a television set full of black folk. Then, on second thought, she was okay with it.

This is my house, and it's not like they can see me, Kay told herself, justifying her nudity. Still, her nipples hardened in the open air as she listened to the interview with Mack, off again, on again, with videos dropped in between. He appeared to be so smug up there on the couch, talking a lot about himself, denying charges that he was a troublemaker and encouraging endearment from the studio audience.

Probably fans, Kay reckoned.

"I'm a really quiet person. A homebody. I trust in the Lord. And, at the end of the day, I'm home looking after my momma . . ."

"Bullshit," Kay said to the TV set, suddenly taking the Jamel Ross/Mack issue personally. "What you really need is your momma to take you over her knee and whup your natural ass real good," she went on, complete with gestures, as if the TV were hearing her loud and clear. Another video came on, with a couple of rappers outnumbered by a couple dozen voluptuous women in thongs, tank tops, and high heels. Kay initially wagged her head and started to change the channel. Then she turned her attention to her own God-given blessings. A moment later she was looking at the bathroom mirror again, her palms underneath her breasts, cupping them and wondering how she measured up in life. Thirty-three didn't feel old, but she could sense that gravity would one day take its toll. Her breasts were still healthy D-cups. They'd endured years of teasing in grade school, they'd grown with her through high school, and they were inevitably the talk of the college campus. But who were they impressing now? Was this mere luggage she'd have to carry through the balance of her life? Who would be the next man to come and pleasure these mammies? Would they be satisfied? "If not, *fuck 'em*," she finally said.

Kay's hands were on her hips now, as she stuck her chest out and held her little belly bulge in, her chest out and proud, with her chin up. Kay sucked her teeth and concluded, "You still got it, girl!" She shook her shoulders slightly and then, as if to compete with the video vixens on the TV, she shimmied, shook her ass, and smoothed her hands along her bare breasts. She made devilish eyes at the mirror, pouted, and then blew a kiss at herself. For an instant, she thought about Jamel. Then she rubbed that thought from her face.

"What's wrong with you, Kay?" Her hands were there on the sink, supporting her as she looked hard and good into her own eyes. "You know he's not for you. Remember? Two different worlds?" Kay let out an exhaustive sigh, unsure of what was going on in her mind. *"Mmm-mmm-mmm,"* she murmured. "You really need to get you some dick."

CHAPTER 7

Jack Bungy was the fifty-something-year-old convict who sported a ponytail and was too frail a man to withstand any physical challenge at this point in his life. Not many people were aware that he was convicted of stealing over 300 million dollars in one of the biggest fraud cases of the decade. And he'd rather they *didn't* know.

From the day he self-surrendered at the entrance of Fort Dix, he felt like he was an endangered species around so much ethnicity. There had to be every nationality and color here, but white men like him were outnumbered a hundred to one. And Spanish seemed to be the preferred language. Club Fed today isn't what it used to be for stockbrokers and judges and bankers. Today, just about anyone could qualify, from low-level drug dealers to shameless child molesters. They were all here at Fort Dix. The trick was to try and realize who you were communicating with while here, because, good or bad, that could make all the difference in the world.

It had been Jack's second day at the institution, while his head was still dizzy from the culture shock (and the idea that he'd have to spend ten years here), when Jamel approached the elder to offer his help. It was nothing, really; just legwork to get some toiletries that hadn't been provided to him. However, Jamel lifting his finger to help was more than anyone else had offered to Jack, including other whites housed in Unit 5852. So once Jack got himself established, and since he recognized Jamel's interest in business, he offered the younger man his subscriptions to the *New York Times* and *Wall Street Journal* once he'd finished looking through them. As far as Jamel was concerned, this marked the beginning of a resourceful relationship.

Further into Jack's first year at Dix, there'd been a time that those promised newspapers had been piling up for a number of days. And since Jack liked to stay confined to his room and hadn't seen Jamel in just as many days, it made him wonder if the young man had gone to SHU for some disciplinary issue, or if he'd even been transferred to another institution. So Jack decided to take a stroll down the hall to room 215, which Jamel had been assigned.

Jack knocked before entering the dorm room and was happy to see that his young acquaintance was still there, lying on his bunk bed and staring at the ceiling. He didn't even see or hear Jack coming into the room.

"You okay?" he asked, tapping Jamel's mattress so as not to startle him.

"Hey, Jack. What's up?" Jamel asked with enthusiasm, and he sat upright in his bunk.

"I suppose I should say 'long time no see,'" said the elder convict.

"Oh. Stupid me. I've been a little under the weather, Jack. Sorry."

"You sick? You need aspirin or painkillers?"

"Oh no—not like *that,* just a little out of it, that's all."

"Anything I can do? Something I can get you?"

"No. I'll be fine, Jack. Believe me. I just need to snap out of it."

"Well, the papers have been piling up, so I brought 'em down. You know how these folks are, nothing but trolls with keys and handcuffs." While Jack was speaking his mind, Jamel was climbing down from his bunk. He then took the stack of newspapers to his locker, stuffed them inside, and hopped back up to his bunk.

This is how it had been going lately. Jamel had fallen way off from his routine of writing various business plans, drawing diagrams and sketches of a dinner club he expected to build when he got home, and when he got up the capital. He'd already completed half of his goal, having developed various outlines, proposals, and many pages of notes; however, if they unlocked the gate now, he was far from ready to go. Sure, he'd leave, but he wouldn't be focused. And that would get him nothing but a one-way ticket back to Fort Dix.

On his bunk, Jamel turned over on his stomach, buried his face in his pillow and his hands underneath his body. This position, no matter what was going on in the world, was where Jamel could escape everything while doing all the dreaming, planning, and plotting he wished.

— — — —

The next important priority after the orderly conduct of convicts is their accountability. There are the periodic head counts every two or three hours after midnight and a couple of times during the daylight. When the lights go out, most convicts are usually sound asleep, and each twelve-man room becomes more or less a gas chamber of conflicting smells. Depending on what the evening meal was, a chorus of gas odors might reflect what was eaten. Some ate more than others. Some ate more beans, eggs, starches, cheeses, and pasta. Some were health nuts and chose soy over all else. But no matter what the meal of the day, it all came out during the late hours of the night in the form of murky, hot, stank air pollution. While their minds rested or visited other worlds, their bodies were no less than parked vehicles, all with their motors still running, all with their tailpipes kicking out one exhaust after another. They snored like bears and ogres; like motorboats and diesel engines. Some just purred like cats. They had great hygiene or they didn't. They had gross habits of snorting, hacking, coughing, or picking their noses or else they did these same things behind the door in the toilet stall so nobody would see. Some men were insecure about themselves and attempted to hide the my-shit-don't-stink mask. Others couldn't care less what the next man thought. This was communal living; deal with it or check in. "Check in" was a popular term, meaning "check into SHU," otherwise known as "the hole," where troubled convicts were segregated away from the general population.

Since Jamel's prison job only required his brief appearance at the yard office, he could sleep most of his days away. After twelve midnight, when the CO was usually on the office phone or outside conversing with other third-shift BOP workers, Jamel would slip downstairs to one of the TV rooms. According to the rules, the televisions and the TV rooms were off-limits during these hours. But, at Fort Dix, every "visitor" was the product of how rules were made to be broken. So convicts would take turns standing as lookouts, while the few other risk takers would camp out on the floor with their Walkman radios and headsets on. The TVs could only be heard through a radio frequency, which kept the TV rooms quiet even during the daytime. And the TVs would immediately be tuned into the "squiggly channels," where the porn channels were distorted for nonsubscribers. However, this was just fine with men who were barred from any female companionship, some for longer than others. As long as the sound wasn't tampered with, this was as good as the real McCoy. Plus, for a second here and there, one could catch the glimpse of a naked breast or some woman being penetrated. Something was better than nothing.

With his hands deep in the pockets of his scraggly gray sweat suit, Jamel tuned in just like the others, listening to the moaning, squealing, sighs, and grunts; the cursing, wails, and cries out for God. And all of it left very little to the imagination and encouraged Jamel's hormones to toss and turn as he thought about his new friend, Dr. Kay.

CHAPTER 8

Jojo and Deadra had had a hard way to go these past four years. To begin with, they were both six and seven months pregnant, respectively, when Jamel was finally sentenced to eighty-four months in federal prison. He hyped them up with talks of appeals and furloughs and satisfactory good time; but in the back of their minds, thanks also to the naysayers, they had to come to terms with the bottom line: eighty-four months was seven years, and a federal prisoner, no matter who he was, had to serve 85 percent of that time before seeing the streets again. That meant the best-case scenario was six years and change. And six years was three times as long as they'd known Jamel. And now, suddenly, they were expected to wait? For what?

It seemed that all they had was each other for a time. The morning sickness. The Lamaze classes and the clinic visits. The Medicare process. The welfare lines. The other single moms and their attitudes in the doctor's waiting area. Just so much to grin and bear, a burden they never prepared for. The next threat to their security was the loss of the penthouse. With Jamel gone and his business shut down, there was no cash flow to maintain the standard of living they'd grown accustomed to. Within the first month of their life without a sole provider, the two women (JoJo was twenty-five and Deadra twenty-eight) had to auction most of their household furnishings, as well as every trace of clothing. The watch collection, the electronics; it all had to go. Considering how they were forced to find a more conservative place to live and that they'd need money for security, two months' rent, the moving expenses, et cetera, JoJo and Deadra didn't do too bad for two women caught up in the struggle. Two women, abandoned during their third trimesters of pregnancy. Within three weeks, they collected $12,000 and moved to a loft in Harlem. They were able to hold on to a couch, a bed, and a kitchen table from the auction so as to have a head start at their new living quarters. They were resourceful with the money, too, knowing they'd have to live off it for at least six months. In the meantime, they consoled each other with talks of who and what their children would become "one day." There was little discussion about Jamel, and of their past as a threesome, since sex was the last thing on their minds. The good times, it seemed, were so good that it hurt to think about them. However, this was the life they lived and the world they chose. And most importantly, there were two newborns on the way.

Jamel phoned his two "friends" a lot at the start of his prison sentence. Adapting to his new life was just as trying as it was for JoJo and Deadra to adapt to theirs. It was a stress-filled uphill battle that they knew nothing about, but which they dealt with regardless. Also Jamel had a different agenda than his friends, more concerned with his surroundings, his safety, and his future as opposed to childbirth, the high telephone bill, and where that next dollar would come from. He even had them indulge in talking dirty to him, to at least reinvent the past for his own sanity. Somehow having his women do and be and say what he needed left him with a sense of power (however imaginary)

that had been stripped from him. But even that had its
limitations.

Just before his sixth year incarcerated, before the
fifth birthdays of son Jamel Jr. (by Deadra) and Sonia,
his daughter (by JoJo), the three got into an angry quar-
rel over the phone as to why there wouldn't be a visit.
As usual, Jamel was adamant and in dire need of affection; that affirmation that love was still there waiting
for him outside of those prison fences and constantine
razor wire. The women were just not up for the ride
and that's all there was to say. An hour and a half each
way, kids in tow, plus all the security measures to go
through before the visit was all too much to bear just
to kiss and hold Jamel and eat coin-machine foods together. At the same time, all the prisoners were having
these on-again, off-again quarrels with their families.
The BOP phone system had installed new rules that
permitted only fifteen minutes per hour and only after
4:00 p.m. count (unless it was legal business or emer-
gencies). All of this was confusing at first: how family,
friends, or whoever needed to "press five" in order to
accept the call, or 7 "to decline the call." And there
were numerous occasions when the message was misunderstood and the 7 was pressed instead, disabling

any future calls until someone in the administration office could fix it. Add to that a notarized letter was needed to correct such a situation. All told, the phone system was more of a discouraging activity than one that was meant to, so to speak, "keep the family ties."

This problem with the phone was eventually a problem of Jamel's. He guessed that one of the kids got to the phone and pressed the wrong button. But even so, Jamel had no way of knowing what had happened and for weeks he was getting the same electronic message: "Your phone call was not accepted." Jamel was left to imagine and to write angry letters. They were never returned to sender, nor did he receive replies. So he was left to believe there was a wall up between him and his loved ones. And there was only one way to deal with this: Handle it. Even if it hurt so bad to feel rejected, and that his people back home didn't know his pain, and that he desperately needed to feel love so that he could strive to be a better man, the bottom line was, "*Fuck it*. It's hard, so *handle it*." He'd hear all the young women calling into the radio station on his Walkman radio, telling their boyfriends and husbands to "hold on," to "be strong," and to look forward to that next visit. They'd be so sexy on the radio, making all kinds of innuendos and promises of passion-filled homecomings, and they'd recite poems of love and affection. They'd dedicate songs by R. Kelly, Maxwell, the Isleys, and Kelly Price, and they'd make tearful apologies. But all the while, at least in his mind, Jamel would imagine it was him they were talking to. When the emotions were too much and too soupy, Jamel would turn to the weaker signal and listen to Kia Renee on "The Touch," imagining her as his surrogate wife; a substitute for all he needed and all he ever wanted in a woman. Kia Renee was so intimate in his ear each night with her warm and saucy voice. She was his seductress and his muse and his therapist all hidden in one radio personality.

For a different means of affection, Jamel began to correspond with female prisoners. And as a result, for almost two years, the mail flowed consistently. The women behind bars seemed to understand most what he was going through and they recognized his true potential as it was expressed in his own words and details. But his angle was to give them just what he was missing. Just as he needed compassion, he gave that same thing to them. Just as he felt lonely, he gave them the attention by pouring his heart into numerous letters—mail they weren't getting (for whatever reasons) from their people back home. In return, dozens of female prisoners from all over the country gave Jamel the same love.

It was Tammy who responded to Jamel's innermost feelings and filled his heart and his mind with fresh imagination.

Tammy wrote: "It's due time that I tell somebody I love them. And, regardless of the distance and barriers between us, I want to hold you. I feel as if I waited forever to feel a love so deep inside of me." Tammy also said that she didn't see Jamel as a stubborn male unable to see love that was staring right at him. She said that the love he needed was right there "inside of me." Tammy pulled no punches and wrote all of this without giving Jamel a photo. He had sent her a photocopy of his image—a publicity photo he took with a singer who had come by one of his Yonkers talent shows back in the day—but nothing tangible like a Polaroid that men and women cherished behind bars. Nevertheless, the two wrote back and forth, sometimes two or three times a week, building something out of nothing. Tammy said things she felt Jamel wanted to hear and Jamel did the same for her. As long as there was a mail call, Jamel always had something to look forward to. So long as she planted lipstick kisses and perfume in her letters, it served the purpose. Tammy was just what Jamel needed. And soon, other convicts were coming to Jamel for a "hook up." When one guy got a letter and a photo from a woman, the word quickly spread, and dozens of others were coming to Jamel with commissary in exchange for his newfound services.

May 24th, 2000

Jay, what's up, baby? How are you? Fine, I hope. Me, I'm doing fine. It's always a pleasure to hear from you, and to know that you're okay. Now, let me get into your letters. First, thank you for the flicks. (Finally!) You know I had to show them off. Mad compliments too! I know you told me you wanted other pen pals, so I told my girls and they said, "Hell yeah!" "Whatever! Hook me up!" So, who are you talking about—that one of your guys wrote to but never got a response? Juana said that she somehow misplaced one guy's letter, so she said please tell him to write her again. Who else is slacking? Let me know so that I can handle that. Brenda said that she hasn't heard from you, and to please write her. (I think she really loves you!) I hope you'll be able to handle all of this pussy when you get home! (Smile, giggle, lipstick)

So, in your letter, you said you liked my photo and hairstyle. I have that bedroom look, huh? Did you like the last fantasy I sent you? If you like this one (enclosed), I'll keep 'em cummin', I'm down for whatever. You know me; anything to please you, Daddy. (Smile) I told all the girls about you wanting to holla at them personally and they said okay. If you want me to, I'll jot down their numbers and let you hit them off directly. I'm about to take some more flicks—hope you'll be able to catch up. (Smile)

Yes, I'm happy you made my (photo) request a reality. You asked me who Nicole and Sarah are. They are friends of mine. I work with Nicole, and Sarah and I hang out most of the time. What else would you like to know about them? Stay tuned.

By the way, I loved the fantasy story you sent me! My girls keep askin' me for more of your work. So, you need to handle that. Note: There's a lot of new females here, too. Another thing; send me some guys' names and numbers and I can pass 'em on, love. I know this thing is bigger than you and I, that's why

I'm so game. Take care, and know that I got mad love for you, baby. w/b/s Tammy

PS: Read the enclosed, I was thinking of you when I wrote it. Tell me what you think!

"No More Clothes" by Tammy

You are home from a long hard day at work and all you have on your mind is me. Your muscles ache and your back hurts. You can't wait to get home to take a nice hot relaxing bath and have me there to take away all of your problems. As you open the door, you do your normal routine; check the mail and go to the refrigerator for a nice cold brew. On the fridge, I left you a note: Dear Love, your bath awaits you, just as I do. So, come to the bathroom for a candlelit bath and the time of your life. I'm going to relax you, massage you and love you. By the way, grab the bottle of Moët in the bucket of ice, and watch your step. I left a path of rose petals on the floor that will lead you to paradise . . .

Jamel's eyes were wide with excitement as he read more into Tammy's letter. Meanwhile, Box and Twan eased ever closer to him to look over his shoulder as usual.

> Of course, you're following instructions, Jay. And while you're following the rose petals, I have on music to fit the moment. And you can hear Meli'sa Morgan's version of "Do Me Baby" playing as you reach the top landing of the steps. There's another note on the floor that reads, "Take off your clothes." You're following my instructions, but you can also smell my bubble bath and incense. The room is dim with candlelight and I'm sitting on the edge of the Jacuzzi wearing a thong and matching bra set. I'm also wearing my fuck-me pumps and I have two wineglasses in my hand. My hair is pinned up in Chinese sticks with the scent of Cristalle all over my body. As you approach, the song changes to "Tease Me Tonight" by Guy. You greet me with a kiss and step into our bubble-filled Jacuzzi and we have a Moët toast. After a moment of casting my unlimited promises into your eyes, I take your hand and lead it to a position between my legs. I slowly massage your temples, neck, and shoulders as your body melts

under the touch of my caring hands. Can't you feel my hands smooth against your chest of velvet steel?

We face one another and I straddle your lap, I lather your body, and I can see you enjoying it. Eventually the music changes once again, and "Freak Me Baby" is encouraging me to stand and dance before you. I'm slow grinding, swerving my hips, calling your attention to my every body part. My hand plays with my chest, belly, and navel, while at the same time I perch my foot up on the edge of the tub with my back toward you. I know you're getting a real good look at my voluptuous ass, and I seize the moment to slowly remove my thong . . .

At the moment, Jamel didn't realize that the room went quiet and that the evening's mail call had stopped. This had happened in the recent past when the pool table got a little too loud, so the rules changed and instead of mail call being at a table to the rear of the room, whichever CO was on duty began using the pool table itself to work from, where separate stacks were organized for magazines and newspapers and for legal and personal mail. But a loud game of pool couldn't compare with the excitement that some of Jamel's mail could bring. A little loud in the corner of the room, Jamel didn't realize that many of the convicts standing by the mail call were suddenly looking in his direction, upset that he was holding up the possibility that they, too, might get some good news.

"Ahh, do you mind back there?" It was nothing new; a warning from the CO. "I could do this later, if you guys want." The CO's threat called up a bunch of sighs and grunts from the others in the room.

Jamel put his hand up, sort of apologizing and agreeing all at once. But as soon as the smoke cleared, his eyes shot right back to Tammy's little fantasy.

I undo my bra and my breasts are relieved, but my nipples are so hard they're slightly aching. I'm still dancing, now with my hands over my head, and I can't believe the I-can't-wait-to-fuck-you expression on your face. So I cut the shit to lower myself so that I can straddle you. I take your face into my hands and I begin to tongue-kiss you deeply. But I'm also paying close attention to your neck, shoulders, and ears. I work my way down to

*your left nipple, sucking and teasing and tugging
at it with my teeth . . . I'm working my magic and
making you feel damn good. Then I do the same
to your right nipple, until eventually I'm tenderly
kissing and licking your chest. I can feel your bulge
below is throbbing against my belly, practically
throwing little punches at me. And now I can't
wait to grab that monster! Do you like the way I
take your pulsating head between my lips, Jamel?
And I'm not being too anxious about it, either. Just
a little welcome party for my boo, to familiarize
you with the warmth of my hot, wet mouth. I can
see and feel your veins, and how your shaft is telling me that you're more than ready for the next
level . . .*

"Keep the noise *down* over there! This is the *last*
warning. One more time, and I'm gonna stop mail call!
Now try me." The CO forced the issue and you could
hear a pin drop in the game room. Jamel realized the
insensitivity here, how selfish he was enjoying the hell
out of this mail and at the same time interfering with
the others. So this time he told his sidekicks to hold
him down and look out for further mail. Meanwhile,

Jamel left the game room for the hallway. It was nothing *but* noise out there, and it would all be blocked out by what his pen pal Tammy had written.

Obviously, you must be lovin' this, because you're growing so big in my mouth! I'm gagging, Jamel. Gagging on your dick! Can you hear the sounds from deep in my throat? God, this meat feels good in my mouth! Okay, okay, I'll be easy like you say. I know, I know. I want this to last, too. Plus, I don't want to give you too much all at once. Let me take the head between my lips . . . you like that? I do want to venture to that most exclusive area. Hope you don't mind. I'm gradually teasing my way down your foreskin, to your swollen balls. I gently place them into my mouth and I juggle them between my tongue and gums. I find myself sucking your dick once more, pulling back and forth at it, tempting you to explode. When you can't take it anymore, you pull my hair so that I'm forced to look into your eyes. Damn, you look sexy, Jamel. And you don't have to say a word, because I can read you loud and clear.

You've let my hair go and you've instructed

me to "sit on your dick" facing you. My hair has fallen onto your shoulders and my face is buried into the crook of your neck as you muscle your way into my diamond mine. Oh shit! I'm a little tight there, Daddy. Please go . . . easy on me. I'm almost crying in your ear, but it's like you don't hear me because there's no mercy in your drive. To make this thing better I sit up so that I can let my own spittle fall between us. I can only hope it will be more lubrication to make this a better fit. After all, I know this was a hard day for you and that you want to let go of some frustration. Oh, and I love that cocky attitude. Like, you're not here to do any of the work. No problem. I got you, Daddy . . . come on, take me! Oh yes! That feels so good! I'm gonna ride you like a cowgirl, Daddy. Oh! You're more than that! You're a bronco! Look at how my back arches; that means you're up in there real good, Daddy! Oh, give it to me! All of it!

I'm kissing you hard on the mouth now, just to let you know this is not only about having a good fuck. I love you! I love your monster in me! And I know you're ready to come, big time! But not *just yet. I'm enjoying watching you and how you're trying to hold back from finishing me off. What, Daddy? You want me to turn around so that you can take me from behind? No problem. I'll just bend over the Jacuzzi like this . . . or how about we get out of the tub and go to the floor; may as well. I could get down on my knees there on that comfortable, plush rug. Okay, you must be reading my mind. I didn't know you were gonna manhandle me like that! Okay, Daddy. Now that I'm on all fours on the bathroom floor, grab my love handles. Yes. Yes, right there. Oh yes, I definitely have all of you. And now you have me thrashing around frantically. Harder! My head and hair are swinging all over the place. Faster! I know you're about to come because something fierce is pounding inside of me. Oh, you gorilla! Ohhhh, you gladiator! Take that pussy. Yes, Daddy. Yes, it's yours! I'm yelling at the top of my lungs. And now, without warning . . . whew . . . I sigh and I whimper. It's a great feeling to satisfy you again.*

Whenever Jamel received letters from the female prisoners up in Danbury, he'd share them with one and all. It made him feel good to make his boys feel good. And because these were women he'd never met, and never planned to meet, sharing them was no biggie. There was nothing to lose.

"You gonna live out her fantasy, dog?"

"I'll do everything except the kiss," Jamel replied. "Ain't no way I'm kissin' where my dick's been." The trio snickered and continued to mill over Tammy's steamy pages.

"Yo, Jay. How come I can't be down?" asked Gliss, the B-more cat who worked up at the commissary.

"Twenny mackerels for you, Mr. CD Players Are Now in the Commissary."

Gliss sucked his teeth and said, "Stop playin'."

Box pulled Jamel away from Gliss, rolling his eyes as he asked, "Whatchu gonna do with these girls after you leave here? Don't you already got two at home?"

"The more the merrier," Jamel said, not so convinced himself. It had been months since he'd received any communication from the girls back home.

"Just let me get a couple, Jay-dog. You know I got like five more calendars to do. But you goin' home in like six months," Box said.

"I'll hook you up. I gotcha," affirmed Jamel. "I'ma

make sure shit is correct for you, the rest of your bid, cuz you *know* we gonna work together when you hit the street. I always need a monster like you, cuz you never know."

"I'll whup a nigga's ass."

"We'll talk about it, Box. Your muscles are only a deterrent. We ain't beatin' people up for a livin'. We only do small talent show. Local shit, feel me? We hardly had one argument, much less a fight."

"I feel you. Just put me down."

Just as Jamel nodded, his name was called once again. The corrections officer's voice carried from the game room just as the door swung open. And Jamel popped right in there.

As soon as Jamel saw the heavy handwriting he knew who it was. He thought, Oh shit, as he ripped open the envelope.

CHAPTER 9

Jamel waited for a few moments on a bench in the Fort Dix yard. He was collecting his thoughts in peace while it seemed all of the rest of the prison environment was swirling around him at full speed. Behind his left shoulder were two housing units. Behind his right shoulder was the prison hospital where every last convict had to pass through for a physical exam upon orientation. The only time to see them again was upon leaving. But everything else was a long wait and a pill of some sort that you had to qualify for. To his right was Unicor, the manufacturing plant that produced everything from furniture to work clothing, much of which was sold in the public marketplace while the men who worked in the plant got paid eleven cents per hour. To his left was one of two chow halls, the feeding facility for the entire institution. During three meals, corrections officers posted up at the entrance and frisked convicts at random. Meanwhile, inside (especially during lunch) the institution's administrative staff, including associate wardens (AWs) and even the warden himself, could be approached in person with issues relating to a convict's stretch. Depending on the day, a warden might or might not be helpful. The bottom line was you received a prison sentence from some judge in some state, somewhere in the country. They sent you here to do your time. Everything else was irrelevant. Arguing your case before the gatekeepers didn't make you a free man. It didn't even give you hope. "Do your time," the saying goes, "but don't let it do you." Still, this was a big show during most every appearance; one that Dr. Kay was sometimes a part of.

Jamel was waiting for her this morning. When he saw her glide down the compound toward her office, he didn't bother to acknowledge her. He merely watched her. He assessed her and thought her walk to be less than affirmative this morning and guessed that she knew where she was headed, but that she was not exactly thrilled with why. He assumed that this was a miserable job for her. Maybe today would be different.

Dr. Kay stepped into the chapel, the same building that housed the psychology department. And Jamel gave her a couple of minutes to get herself together. He was on time; she wasn't. And he could use that if he so wished; her being late and making little of his value and his time. And then he laughed at the thought of playing mind games with a psych: Better not.

It was a bitterly cold Tuesday morning and Jamel was ready to come in from the cold.

＿ ＿ ＿ ＿

Waiting in the hallway just outside her door, Jamel peeked through her narrow window so that she wouldn't notice. Dr. Kay was adjusting her bra straps, she slipped off her pumps, and rubbed her hands together for some instant warmth. Then she started a coffee machine before checking her makeup in a small hand mirror until she was content. Now Jamel knocked.

"Come in," said the doctor. "Good morning, Jamel. How are you?"

Humbled, Jamel didn't exactly make eye contact with Dr. Kay. But he nodded in response.

"So we're together again. I know it's been a minute, but I had a little vacation time, and then I had you scheduled a few weeks ago, but a surprise staff meeting came up and I had to reschedule you. Is everything okay? Staying out of trouble?"

"Tryin'," Jamel answered as he got comfortable on the couch. He noticed Dr. Kay was wearing a knee-length skirt and a matching blue top under a dark blue blazer. Her neckline was just below the collarbone; enough skin to excite Jamel's interest.

"So last we spoke we were gonna come up with some ideas to focus on . . . to free your mind."

Jamel now understood what she was looking at on the computer at her desk. She had notes on him? On her computer?

He challenged her. "How'd you remember that? I'm not all laid out in one of your notebooks, am I?"

"What makes you think I don't remember, Jamel? What do you think, I haven't been paying attention? That I haven't been doing my job? We've had almost ten meetings."

"I guess I underestimated you," said Jamel.

"Well, don't. I'm concerned about you, Jamel. I want you to get through this time successfully; to go home and make those important *contributions* you spoke of. To take care of those children."

Jamel was visibly discouraged.

"What's wrong?" she asked.

"Doc, I haven't heard anything about the situation back home."

"Nothing?"

Jamel wagged his head.

"They should've at least written. How old are they now?" she asked.

"One should be six years old."

"That's not right. You have to be in touch with your children. Even if it's by phone. Is there anything I can do?"

Jamel pictured the doctor visiting his ex-lovers JoJo and Deadra. He pictured her bitch-slapping at least one of them and putting a foot in somebody's ass, telling them how wrong they were about this and that. The image made him snicker.

Dr. Kay was assertive and went on to say, "I'm serious. Would you like me to arrange a phone call? And if you don't feel up to it, I can do it."

Jamel felt himself slipping deeper into her suggestion and he wondered if this wasn't her just being nosy.

Plus, he was lying straight to her face. Deadra had recently written him, apologizing for everything. She wrote in large print: "PLEASE DON'T EVER DOUBT HOW MUCH I LOVE YOU! I have just been in this space where I needed to think about myself (and our child) for a while. Both JoJo and I are going through the same things, but she's okay. We're doing this together, Jay. JoJo sends her love. The children are just fine (pictures enclosed) and they miss you. They ask for you all the time . . ."

Jamel shook the spell and returned to the moment. "Now didn't we say I should focus on ideas to free my mind? I mean, I love my children and all—love 'em to death. But I can't go around beating myself in the head about it. If the woman, or the women won't act correctly . . . if they don't appreciate the total man that I am, then I can't cry over it, can I? I have to keep on truckin'. Sure, I think about the kids, but to an extent you have to understand that it gets painful. It's natural for a father to want to be with, hear from, and see his children—I know that because I feel sick sometimes. All this baby momma drama," Jamel lied. "You've heard of that, I'm sure."

"Too many times. And always, the children are the ones who suffer. Still, with all the cases I've heard of, communication was always the answer. To air your feelings and maybe focus on some priorities and—"

"Sorry to cut you off, Doc. But my priorities are right here, right now. Staying alive in here is a priority. Not going crazy is a priority. Planning my future is a big priority, yes. But the moment you lose yourself in your dreams in here, you could be chewed up and spit out. My life is the only priority right now, because without that those children won't have a daddy to come home. Everything I do at every minute right here where I am means everything to those children and their futures. This, Doc, is the ultimate sacrifice."

Nothing was said for a time. Kay took a deep breath and got up to pour herself a cup of freshly brewed coffee.

"Coffee?" Jamel declined and Kay was at once glad for the coffeemaker and how it served as a buffer from one part of this session to the next. Those were some strong thoughts he'd dropped on her, as if his one explanation was the definition of all the hundreds of convicts she'd ever met with; all those who couldn't or weren't able to express their pains and anguish. Still, it was deathly silent in the office. Dr. Bash wouldn't be in until 10:00 a.m. And there were no other workers in the psychology department as yet. Even the compound was quiet but for a PA announcement here and there: "Ten-minute move! Ten-minute move! All convicts to their assigned locations!" It was an announcement that didn't apply to Jamel since he was scheduled for this appointment, with a notation in the prison database.

"So tell us what to do." Kay meant to ask a question, but it came out more like a suggestion. Suddenly she was unsure of herself; a mistake in this line of work. "What, ah . . . what activities would you suggest to help you through this? To make you feel good and keep your mental health during these otherwise uncertain times?"

"Can I speak from my heart?"

"Has that ever stopped you before today? Go'won," said Kay, with a slight adjustment in her seat.

Jamel's breathing stammered. The words were choked back in his throat as he stared at the doctor. Her golden brown hair in that fancy flip style women wore these days. Her outfit so discreet, but to him it also served as a pretty blue packaging of what Jamel assumed was a marvelous prize of female flesh underneath. No shoes on those stocking feet. Her eyes were warm and compassionate, and her lips were no less than sumptuous strawberries. This was how Jamel viewed Dr. Kay, and this was the moment he'd dreamt about. That door of opportunity.

"Uh . . ." he hesitated. "I . . . have a pen pal." Jamel immediately felt relieved to have come up with the answer so quickly. Although it's not what he wanted to say; what he wanted was to plant his lips on hers. He wanted to get his hands on those big round breasts. He even wanted to pull those stockings off and suck her toes until she squealed. Shit! And nobody was around to see or hear all of this possibility. And now his failure to follow through with his imaginings made him slump back on the couch with perspiration built up under his clothes.

"A pen pal?" Dr. Kay asked.

"Right." Jamel paused to buy time. He had to think about the abundance of mail he was already getting and wondered if she knew. Nah, he finally told himself. Then to her he said, "You know, a person who could express themselves to me—a person to whom I can also express *myself* to. Someone to help me *breathe* in here. It's real hard to breathe right now, Dr. Kay."

CHAPTER 10

They set the alarm for 6:00 a.m. and expected to be out of the door and on the road by 6:30, 6:45 at the latest. But for JoJo and Deadra, just as it was for so many others, things didn't quite work out the way they'd planned. It was Sunday, visiting day up at Fort Dix. They hadn't visited Jamel in four months and it felt like forever up until the drive. That long hour-and-a-half drive that grew twice as long with the kids and their shenanigans. But then again, just about everything felt like forever when life was all twisted like this; all backed up, stressed, and confusing because of a man in prison.

Jamel's loved ones had taken this drive down to New Jersey on many occasions since he took the fall.

And in the beginning it was twice as bad since they had to finagle a ride here and there from the fair-weather friends that Jamel had back then. There were still a few of those friends around, like Troy, who sometimes stopped by the apartment to play surrogate father, with Jamel Jr. especially. But besides Troy popping in unannounced, JoJo and Deadra saw themselves as Jamel's only true soldiers, knowing that this was but another battle in this man's war to succeed. Certainly the girls knew the difference between right and wrong, and they were at least aware that the ones who did wrong (when they were caught doing wrong) went to jail. But both had a past that reached back into the hood. They'd heard the many stories of injustice, of corruption in law enforcement, and how the penalties were unbalanced and sometimes downright backward when it came to the less fortunate, minorities, and the underclasses. How could Jamel, who did little more than write funny checks, receive more time than a man who had committed manslaughter? Or more than someone who assaulted, or who burglarized? These issues were much too complex to dwell on for a black woman who knew not. Like many others who walked in their footsteps day after day, week after week, and month after month,

JoJo and Deadra were left only to cope, to struggle, and sometimes against their wishes, to withstand the majority of what was left behind—the black man's burden.

Having cleared the security check, including the almighty computer files, the walk-through and hand-held metal detectors, and the roving eyes of various corrections officers, the two adults and two children joined a half-dozen others to step into a foyer (which looked something like a gas chamber) that was sealed off before another door slid open to permit their final entry into Fort Dix. The children were the first to shoot out into the open air, hopping and dancing with joyous anticipation through a small courtyard and patio that led from the administration building's control room to the prison visiting room.

"Hurray! We're gonna see Daddy!" little Sonia cried. It was a moment that made JoJo look at Deadra, wagging her head at how magical it was: a child's love for her daddy. These kids didn't have a care in the world and their bubbly attitudes somehow diffused the pain, if only for an instant. The real deal here was the "grown folks' business," like the pressure of time constraints, the repressed emotions, and the pent-up rage at the system they seemed to be caught up in.

Inside the visitors' building was nothing more than a hospital waiting room, or worse, like the waiting room at the local clinic, complete with all the noise, babies crying, and kids roughhousing. If not for the ounce of affection and emotion they looked forward to from the man they both loved, JoJo and Deadra could have done without yet another group of mothers and their unruly children all shut in amidst plastic chairs, vending machines, and unfriendly overseers.

There was a brief wait during which the family situated itself among the chairs, ever aware of the cameras up in those black globes on the ceiling, as well as the uniformed officers monitoring the vast room from behind that huge desk. Periodically a door at the rear of the room would swing open and one, two, or three convicts would march out in search of their loved ones. They couldn't miss how some women clung to their men in those first moments, or how they didn't. Some indulged in that long "I miss you" kiss, and for others it was a peck on the cheek for old times' sake. Or maybe for the children's sake.

"JoJo, we gotta represent, baby. It's been a while," said Deadra.

"I swear, he's gonna be pissed. I don't know if I can put up with his attitude."

"Just shake it off, girl. Remember what we talked about? The struggle? Sacrifices?"

"I'm tired of struggling, Dee. Sometimes I just want this all to end."

"Oh. And I *don't*?" Deadra reached over and rubbed JoJo's shoulder. "Come on, babe. You can do this. We owe him that much." Before JoJo could respond, Jamel Ross Jr. shouted, "Daddy, Daddy!"

"DAAADDY!!!" Now, Sonia joined in, following her brother as he sprinted across the floor toward his dad. Jamel lifted his son, then his daughter, and swung them back and forth in his embrace.

"Hi, Daddy," Deadra said in a sensual tone and she stood by waiting her turn. JoJo was just behind her, unable to prevent a smile.

"Okay, okay, stop hogging Santa Claus. Let Mommy have her turn." Deadra eased up and slipped her hands around Jamel's waist. Their lips met and their tongues instantly wrestled for a place inside each other's mouths.

"I'm jealous—you all know how I get," said JoJo with her pout. Jamel ripped away from Deadra and grabbed JoJo for a hungry bear hug. Then he took her mouth with his. All the while, many sets of eyes were on the family. It had to be strange to see how lusty Jamel Ross was with each woman and how they all seemed so cooperative and comfortable with it all.

Jamel was fully aware that others were watching, how he had these two women lined up for a piece of him. He also knew that he couldn't get out of hand with the kissing, or else the COs would turn jealous instead of amazed like they were now. He grabbed at both women and the kids clung to both his legs as he worked his way to their seats.

"Long time, huh?" Jamel said, not necessarily re- quiring an answer.

"Daddy, Mommy said you were coming home soon," said Jamel Jr.

"Does that mean we're not coming here to your job anymore?" Sonia asked.

"No, darling. Soon Daddy will be working at home."

"Does that mean the officers will be coming to our house, too?"

Jamel made eyes at JoJo before he jumped into the conversation.

"No, Jamel Ross. It'll just be me . . ." He tickled his son feverishly. "And you, ya lil' rascal." The six-year-old cackled and tried to wiggle away from his dad. When the worst of the assault was over, Jamel Jr. went back and clung to his father, not wanting to let go. Jamel squeezed his son harder in response and it stayed like that for a moment.

JoJo whispered, "Baby, Sonia's getting jealous."

Jamel suddenly realized that his daughter was being left out and said, "Come-eer, doll. Who's the most beautiful girl in all the world?"

"Sonia."

"That's right," Jamel said and pulled both children in for a big hug. Jamel looked over the children's heads at their mothers. Deadra was wiping away a tear and JoJo had a sad joy about her. It was a bittersweet moment, the stuff that only adults were familiar with. Jamel couldn't help his own eyes becoming wet. After a while, the children went to the playroom, a glass enclosure with a television and Playskool tables in the back. From where Jamel sat between JoJo and Deadra, half a room away, he could keep an eye on the children.

"You miss me?" he asked both of them, his arms pulling them in closer. JoJo propped her head on his shoulder and toyed with his fingers. Deadra had a hand on his head, caressing his scalp, while her other hand was on his thigh.

"Of course, baby. We're not a family without you."

"I wish you would come home and take these damn kids, since you got 'em all hypnotized. I need a damn break," JoJo said.

"How about if I hypnotized you?"

"That, too." JoJo blushed.

"You ain't turned shy on me, have you? Not the girl who likes the spankings . . . not the girl who begs Daddy to talk dirty to her." JoJo hid her face in Jamel's collarbone.

"And what about you, boo? You miss this dick in your mouth? Huh?" Jamel gave her shoulder a squeeze as he said this.

"Mmm-hmm . . . you know I do."

"You think you still got it, baby?"

"I think I remember how." She smiled a shy smile.

"I'm gonna be a virgin when I get home. You think you all can turn me out?"

"We're gonna freak your ass for a week straight—maybe try some new things."

"Oh yeah? Something we haven't done before?"

JoJo reached in her bra, both sides. "I forgot. These are for you. A lil' gift." Jamel was suddenly looking at two pieces of Trident gum that JoJo pulled out and put on the table.

"O-kay" Jamel said, stunned.

"I know you used to like gum so much; remember when we used to share the same piece?"

"Y-yeah. But do they allow you to bring that in here?"

"'Course not. That's why I snuck it in my bra, silly."

"Oh," Jamel said, but then changed subjects, wanting desperately to keep the discussion about sex.

"So tell me, have you two been naughty while Daddy's been away?"

"Very."

"How naughty? You first, Dee. What's the last thing JoJo did that was nasty?"

"The other day."

"Oh yeah?" Jamel gave a mock-scolding look.

"She took out the ski mask again."

"No shit."

"I was sleeping."

"Were not."

"Anyway . . . I *was* sleeping, but JoJo, with her slut self, was *licking* me. She woke me up and scared the shit out of me. I thought I was being robbed."

Jamel and JoJo laughed.

"Then what?"

"I didn't think that shit was funny. She apologized, but I said, 'No bitch, you owe me slave hours.'"

"You all still do slave hours like we used to?"

"Yup."

"So what did ya make her do, Dee?"

"I rolled over on my stomach and I had that bitch lick my asshole."

"Whooo . . . bad *girl*, JoJo."

"And she fuckin' loved it, too."

"Jay?!?" Deadra said, indicating the bulge in his khaki pants.

Jamel read her thoughts and said, "Oh well, too bad you can't suck it, baby." Deadra looked around, up at the officers' station, then she made a swipe with her hand, grabbing Jamel's erection quickly.

"So JoJo . . . what has Dee done to be naughty?"

"I caught her—"

"*Jo!*"

"Oh? Big secret, Dee? Caught her what, Jo?"

"Caught her with the Jamel."

"The Jamel?"

"That's the dildo we named after you . . ."

"Excuse me," said a man's voice. Jamel looked quickly in front of him. Two officers stood there. "We're going to have to ask you to come with us, sir."

"Huh?" Jamel said. "What's up?"

"The lieutenant wants to see you, sir. Up at the desk. You'll need to come with us." The corrections officers looked a little uncomfortable but were steadfast in their mission.

"What's wrong, Officer?" asked Deadra.

"What's happening?" JoJo said simultaneously.

"I'm sorry, he's gonna need to—"

"It's okay, babe. Easy. I'll be right back. Everything's gonna be fine."

JoJo got up to retrieve the children. Whatever was going down, it didn't feel right. She felt the need to protect the children. Meanwhile, Jamel was escorted through the throngs of onlookers and it was a big exhibition as he walked up to the lieutenant.

"What's up, LT?"

"You're gonna need to tell your guests that the visit is terminated."

"What's wrong?"

"We're terminating the visit."

"Why?"

"I'm not at liberty to discuss that right now."

"I don't understand. What's this about?" Even though Jamel showed mild argument, he knew from his observations over the past years how this worked. Do as they ask. This is *their* game. *Their* rules. Don't shake the tree or go against the grain. Whatever this is, it'll blow over.

"Baby, I have to go. They're terminating the visit."

"Why?"

"What's wrong?"

"It's just best that you go. Don't make a scene, baby." Jamel kissed and hugged both women in a haste to disappear. He kissed his children and spun off with the two officers on either side of him. It was as though he were being arrested again, only *inside* the jail.

— — — —

They made a bigger deal than usual of the strip search. Usually some cops didn't even *do* a strip search; maybe because they didn't want to have to sleep with all of those images of men's assholes dancing around on the walls of their minds. But now the two cops both stood by to watch and direct Jamel to do the whole lift-your-balls-and-turn-around-and-bend-over-and-spread-'em bit. After he got dressed, Jamel was escorted out of the visiting room, outside along a sidewalk to the lieutenant's office, where he waited for half an hour before he was finally addressed.

"Come with me," a cop told Jamel and he followed the portly figure through the makeshift police station. A few doors down the corridor, Jamel could see he was about to be addressed by the captain, the man with the godly control over the prison compound. Jamel saw a back room with riot gear. In the captain's office there were photos of him with this person and that, and plaques of this and that achievement, as well as shelves of loose-leaf binders.

"Mr. Ross, do you know why you're here? Why we terminated the visit?"

"No. But whatever it is, you all are sadly mistaken." Jamel wondered if the kisses were too engrossed or if they saw Deadra touching his dick.

"Well, would it surprise you to know that we have videotape that says different?"

"I really don't know what you mean."

"My officers observed your visitors giving you contraband and we also have you swallowing it."

"Is that what this is about?" Jamel let out an audible sigh of relief. "I thought . . ." he chuckled while saying, "this was about kissing or something I did out on the compound, man." Jamel was seated as he learned this and he sat back now, wagging his head in relief. The captain always appeared to be so out of place at Fort Dix, as though he belonged in *GQ*, or as host of *America's Most Wanted*. He had that serious-as-stone look in his eye; the kind of eyes that flashed an all-knowing expression, even if they didn't know all. Surely, Jamel knew, this guy was smart enough to recognize a mistake when it was made.

"That was gum my wife brought, trying to surprise me. I guess she was trying to be sly about it, but she didn't mean no harm."

"Well, what if I told you that both women were being questioned by the feds."

"They can handle it. Nothing new where we come from."

"And you're saying no drugs were exchanged. And you didn't swallow anything?"

"Captain, I didn't even eat the gum. It's been so

long since I've had any that I lost a taste for it. I just left it there."

"So the videotape is lying."

"Basically. I don't do drugs, Captain. Never touched them in my life. *Never.*"

The captain did some thinking and stared at Jamel. To that end he said, "Well, I'll have to lock you up and have you give me four shits. If everything's okay, I'll let you out—no problem." Jamel already imagined the extents of which the captain spoke, but was prepared to go the distance to prove everyone wrong. He guessed that it might take a day or two.

"Do you have to pack up my belongings? Because when this is over you'll see I'm telling the truth. I mean, there's no sense in disrupting my whole locker when I'll be returning shortly."

"I'll see what we can do," the captain replied before Jamel was escorted to the hospital, where an officer was assigned to watch him. The officer was given directions once Jamel was locked in a holding cell. The room had a large picture window and a steel door with a trap through which food trays could be passed.

"He wears nothing but his underwear and T-shirt. One paperback book. No writing tools and no property. The food tray is removed, along with forks and spoons, as soon as he's finished eating. When he wants to brush his teeth you have to provide him with the toothbrush and paste and he must be watched. When he has to defecate, the lieutenant must be called to be present . . . any questions?"

"Nope."

"Okay. Keep an eye on him and record everything in the logbook and, oh . . . and the light stays on."

Jesus Christ, thought Jamel. And the wait was on. The cops worked eight-hour shifts. All of those assigned took the position as overtime. Therefore, Jamel realized, that additional money was being spent all because of him. Moreover, these guys had to watch him take a shit four times. The thought alone felt as if he was smacking his captors in the face. Still, Jamel cursed JoJo for not following the visitors' rules. Doing so would've avoided all of this.

CHAPTER 11

News traveled fast at Fort Dix. However, in the case of Jamel Ross, suspected small-time drug smuggler, it didn't have to travel far to reach Dr. Kay Edmondson. Not only is the hospital in the same building as the chapel and psychology department, but there are myriad doors and passages that are the arteries and veins of the facility. Naturally Dr. Kay Edmondson had the necessary keys to move through the building at will.

"He's been sleeping a lot," the on-duty CO told Kay when she showed up in the deserted hospital wing on Monday evening. It was just past 5:00, a time that she would've been home, or at least on her way home.

"How long will he be here?"

"Until he, ahh, ya know, does his thing four times."

"*Oh,*" Kay said, with a peculiar expression that followed.

"Say, do you think you, I, uh . . ."

"Spit it out, buddy."

"Could you cover me for a few minutes? I need to go to the head myself. The wife fed me lasagna last night and my stomach's not agreeing."

"Oh my. What do I need to do?"

"Nothing really. He's sleeping so we won't have any surprises."

"Oh."

"Otherwise, I won't be more than fifteen minutes."

"Fine by me. Take your time."

"There's a *People* magazine here if you wanna read."

"Thanks. You go on."

— — — —

Jamel swore he was seeing things. First of all, the light was turned off now in the cell. That caused his eyelids to relax and eventually he looked through watery eyes at what he reckoned was a mirage.

"Hey there," Dr. Kay said through the glass. She could see Jamel well enough with the hallway light casting its hazy glow into the cell. "I thought you might be more comfortable with the light off." Jamel thought of a joke, wondering, if comfort was an option, could she come and give him a back massage; but he kept it to himself. Suddenly conscious of his lack of clothing, Jamel checked his boxers to be sure nothing was hanging out, and he stepped over to the window for a closer chat.

"You heard what happened?"

"Mmm-hmm," she said as she nodded. "Sorry to see you like this."

"I never touched drugs in my life, Doc. Too scared, I guess."

"They're probably a little paranoid," she said. "A lot comes in through the visiting room. We got a lot of bad publicity last year for the very same concerns."

"So I'm a trade-off for someone's warped sense of securing this place? There's so many security faults here it's a shame. The fence is close enough to the road that a gun could even be thrown over the fence— forget the videotapes and cell phones that made it over. And speaking of the fence, when there's a thunderstorm they cut off the sensors around the whole perimeter. So what's secure here and *what's not?*"

Kay shrugged. It wasn't her fault, being just another pawn in the game. Then she said, "At least you finally got your visit. How are your children?" she asked, slick at changing the subject. Jamel answered her but there was something else he noticed as he stood at the window, a feeling that he chose to go with.

"You know, I've been meaning to ask you . . . do you mind if I call you by your first name? I mean, you call me 'Jay' all the time."

"I . . . I guess. As long as it's not in front of others. You know, we're supposed to keep it on a last-name basis by policy."

"Right. That damn policy again." Jamel injected the swear word intentionally, loosening things up a bit. He put his finger on the glass now, up where Kay's forehead was. He slowly outlined her head. Very slowly. "So . . . what brings you down, Kay?"

"I heard about you, and . . . I was concerned."

"Aw, come on . . . it's almost dinner hour. Shouldn't you be home? Maybe looking after some lucky guy; maybe him looking after *you?* Making you all comfy? Taking off your shoes and, ya know, that whole relaxation bit."

"Oh. Nothing like that at home. Just me and the TV."

"No man? Psssh . . . are you kiddin'? Not Miss Hold Her Head High?"

"Huh?"

"Yeah, I see you out there walkin' the compound, maybe coming and going, or maybe on your way to lunch. The way you walk, I'd swear somebody special was in your life. That somebody was takin' care of that." Jamel was speaking in riddles, a softer way to reference Kay's genitals. His finger was tracing her shoulders now, descending to the breasts.

Kay folded her arms, showing her surprise at Jay's being so bold and direct. But he knew that's what she liked about him. The hint of a bad boy. Of mischief. Perhaps it took this moment, seeing him in his underwear, to reveal certain truths. And that empowered Jamel. He figured, What the fuck. How much lower could I get? He was already standing before this woman in his boxers, just film on his body if she were to look real close. Plus, she was trying so hard not to look at the bulge he had. So he played on that slight insecurity. Where he might've otherwise felt naked and weak, he flipped it and used the circumstance as energy. There was nothing he wouldn't say now.

"I didn't know I came off that way, Jay," Kay said with a chuckle. "And no. Nobody is, *ahem*, 'taking care of this.' *This*—thank you very much—can take care of itself." Jay's finger was stroking the glass close to her waist now, up and down, as though it was her body he was touching.

"You know, Kay, I'm really . . . it's too bad we had to meet under these circumstances."

"Why's that?"

"Well, if, let's say, we met at the park, or maybe if we went to the same college . . ."

"I was seeing somebody in college."

"That wouldn't have mattered to me."

"Oh *really*."

"Not a bit. One thing you already know about me, Kay. I'm unique. And everything I do is unique . . ." Jamel allowed his eyes to gradually cruise up and down the length of her body. *"Everything."*

A shiver went through Kay when he said that. It had been quite a while since a man spoke to her or looked at her like he did. And this man had a pair of iron balls to be so explicit from his position, a prisoner . . . a number owned by the government. It turned Kay on.

"And you know what else? If we did meet under different circumstances, there's nothing I wouldn't do for you."

Kay gasped and said, "A charmer, are we?"

"Well, you always said you like to keep it real. So there it is. And you know what?" Jamel heard keys in the distance. "Regardless of my current circumstances, I can take that experience . . . I can imagine all of that, our meeting . . . me doing things for you . . . and I can lay right there and sleep and smile my ass off. And if nobody was around, the thought might take me to other worlds," Jamel said, with his finger, stroking the glass down low where Kay's thighs met.

Why the hell was she still folding her arms? Why was she all choked up, at a loss for air all of a sudden? Why was her stomach quivering and how could Jay be so cavalier while she was practically melting with desire? Kay had the urge to smoke and she'd never touched a cigarette in her life.

The on-duty CO returned from the bathroom.

"Okay. All better," the CO said, approaching Kay

at the cell window. "Yeah, I was gonna cut the light off, too. Seems so silly him sleeping there under the light like some exhibit. Thanks again," he said and picked up the *People* magazine.

Kay cast another look at Jay lying there on the naked mattress. She knew for sure he was peeping at her under those closed eyelids.

CHAPTER 12

Kay's hospital visit was detrimental in just one way; it kept Jamel asleep, without an appetite, and that meant a longer stay in the isolation unit. More overtime hours for whomever. For Jamel, however, it was bittersweet. He had to remain caged, but the dreams . . . oh man, the dreams! Kay butt naked on all fours . . . Kay with her knees stretched back to her ears . . . Kay on her knees, pulling at Jamel like a milkmaid. After four days, Jamel had provided the required excrement. Each time he did it was eventful, like some bomb experts toiling through his shit with a wooden spatula and plastic gloves. But it was over now. It was time to be released back into the general population. Jamel had been wondering if he'd get his same bed assignment . . .

if the dudes in his room looked out for his property, making sure the officer packed everything. It wasn't easy to get a bottom bunk. Generally, you'd have to wait in line. If someone in the room went home, or went to the hole, or went back to court, then a bed would free up and the convicts in the room would all shift to a more desirable location based on seniority. Musical beds. Before the visit, weeks earlier, in fact, Jamel finally got a bottom bunk. And then he got a new bunkie, some young cat named Red. Word was that Red had been transferred from this prison and that he was unable to program himself or to adjust.

Jamel heard the nineteen-year-old say, "I'm not stupid . . . I already know I'll be doin' time for the rest of my life . . ." It was a statement deep into an ongoing conversation and Jamel was ear hustling as it was. But clearly Red was expecting to come back to prison again and again. It was just how limited his outlook on life was. From that time on, Jamel kept a distance from Red. As best he could, it was just "hi" and "bye." Because this was dormitory-style living and Fort Dix was some ol' college-type setting, the twelve-man rooms were someplace to merely lay your head. It wasn't a place to be twenty-four hours, seven days a week. Who wanted to be around and see the same men every damn minute of the day? Thank God for the great outdoors and some of the other activities on the compound. Upon release, Jamel was told that his property was indeed packed up, contrary to the best that the captain could do, and he had to trek across the compound to pick up the two duffel bags. On the way back to the unit, Jamel passed Red and they acknowledged each other in a way that admitted they were neither friends nor foes.

Back at the unit, the officer assigned Jamel to the same room, same bed. It was the relief he'd hoped for. No one took his bed; or so it seemed. Once he got in the room he immediately saw a problem. The locker he'd had just days earlier had a combination lock on it that wasn't his. Meanwhile the locker beside it was without a lock. It was junked, with remnants of Jamel's property. There were drawings he'd done, pencil sketches that were scrunched up and wrinkled, newspapers and photocopies of important articles.

"The cop threw your shit out on the floor, Jay. He didn't give a fuck. Just said it was too much work and that he wasn't gonna do it."

"Fuck!" Jamel realized that the duffel bags he had weren't complete and almost half of his personal property had been taken. Books. Toiletries. Sweatpants and sweatshirts. His weight-lifting gloves. His drawings for the dinner club he planned to build. "Fuck! Fuck! *Fuck!!!*" he shouted. It was lunch hour, so few convicts were in the building.

"Here's a few books I saved for ya," said Irving, the Hasidic who always picked his nose but who often thumbed his nose at others.

"Thanks," Jamel said. But no thanks, he also thought. Filled with rage and feeling some possessive interest in the locker with the combination lock on it, Jamel took a metal drawer from the abandoned locker and used it to slam open the combination lock. It popped open on the second strike. "Oh shit!" Jamel said, instantly recognizing property that belonged to him. But it wasn't all his, it was his property mixed with someone else's. There were cutouts of Halle Berry, Lil' Kim, and Mary J. Blige toothpasted to the locker's walls. A toiletries caddie that was attached to the inside door of the locker was altered: Jamel's name was blacked out and it said "Red" now.

"Fuck!" Jamel began snatching things out of the

locker that he knew were his. In no time, there was a pile of belongings on the bed, all taken from the locker . . . all stolen, as far as Jamel was concerned.

▬ ▬ ▬ ▬

Ten minutes hadn't passed before Red came into the room. "Whatchu doin' in my locker?" he said with a dumb expression on his face.

"This ain't your locker, kid. It's *my* locker. And this is *my* shit."

"Ain't nothin' yours in there."

"We must be havin' a communication problem . . . *this*? This is mine . . . you *see*? JAMEL ROSS!" Jamel pointed to the inside corner of a *Webster's Collegiate Dictionary*. Red apparently neglected to check the inside of the book when he ripped off the identifiable glossy red cover. Now that Jamel thought about it, Red altered a lot of things to conceal or hide the origin of various items.

"Naw . . . that shit is mine," Red said with every bit of conviction in his tone. Jamel knew there was a big problem here. Things happened superfast from that point. Red turned to close the door. Jamel swung the drawer in an upward motion and caught Red on the brow. It backed the youngster up and he touched his head to find it bleeding. Jay threw the drawer now without a second's wait, and he followed the drawer with a roundhouse kick. Red was thrown back into another bunk bed before falling to the floor.

"I don't want no problems, Red. That shit is *mine*. I'm takin' it back. *Period*." Red was hyper, as though the kick motivated him. He got up. Jamel couldn't make two cents out of what the kid was saying, too absorbed in all the movement. Much too interested in ending this. By the time Red was up, Jamel had the door opened. He wanted no more of this. He wasn't clear where he was going, just that this was wrong and he wanted out. Red lunged at him and pulled Jamel back into the room. Jamel quickly snatched Red into a headlock. The two ended up on the floor wrestling until they both agreed it had gone too far. There was a crowd of convicts at the door now, excited and fixed on the two contenders.

"Man, listen. You wanna steal? You wanna be known as a thief? You can have it. You can have it *all*. You want the rest of my property, too?" Jamel said this for all to hear. Red was silent. Common sense seemed to overcome him. He left the room in a huff.

"Lemme through!" Bones's voice preceded him

and then he appeared, pushing his way through the crowd of onlookers. Red passed him simultaneously.

"Yo! I heard they let you out, dog. What the fuck's goin' on? What's the crowd about?"

Jamel let out an exhaustive moan and said, "Ain't shit. Help me get my property together."

"Ross!" An authoritative voice this time. Jamel wondered if Red went and told the cops. But the counselor had another agenda.

"Heard you just came back. Pack your shit. You're movin' to room two-oh-seven."

Jamel was about to ask why, but his mind calculated that 207, just down the hall, was a two-man room. The revelation was enough to keep his lips zipped.

— — — —

By 4:00 p.m. stand-up count, Jamel was settled in. His locker was all organized. His bed was made with newly issued bedding and he'd jumped in the shower. His new roommate was some old dude named Almonte. It was just as well that the Dominican couldn't speak a lick of English and that Jamel knew only one word in Spanish: amigo. Sometimes no communication was better in such close proximity. On the other hand, respect was a universal characteristic to observe. So, for Jamel, this was gonna be a cinch. No more Red. No more Irving picking his nose. No more conflicting gases from eleven different men. No more nothin'. Peace of mind. Privacy. Jay didn't care why, just that he was free.

"Mail call!" shouted the officer, and convicts gathered around the pool table where mail was quickly sorted for distribution. An unusual adrenaline also filled the air thanks to a certain fight, and also because of a certain person having come out of solitary confinement. Not to mention the biggest plus: Jamel's pen pal letters.

"You get any mail while you were on lock?" Twan asked.

"Nah. Maybe they held it back or somethin'. I could definitely use a good mail day right now."

"You ain't the only one," said Gliss. Jamel shook his head, wondering where the hell he came from.

"Whassup, Jay," said Roy, who'd just shown up. Jamel looked around the room. Not much changed since he'd been gone. And yet convicts smiled at him as if to congratulate and praise his return. There was Pat, the white dude with the gray and white ponytail and busted teeth who was always trying to get over on the government. There was Big Ali with Mark and X, all of them doing pull-ups on the bar in the corner. A little showing off mixed with a little focus, all in the presence of a couple hundred convicts. There was Raheem, doing twenty-eight years for a bank robbery. J.R. was a small-time smuggler, and beside him was Chuck, the pilot who claimed innocence but who bragged about all the kilos he'd brought into the country in his private Cessna. Rick was a *GQ* cover type; a superintendent who dealt drugs to many of the residents in the buildings he managed. Fonz was an older man, an accountant who played with numbers a bit too much and who had a distinctive Southern drawl. There were just so many drug dealers, bank frauds, credit frauds, insurance frauds, and gunrunners—men of every color and size. Half-blind, crippled, and crazy, the BOP was accepting applications.

"Ross!" called out the officer and a few sets of eyes followed the envelope as it was passed forward. Jamel opened it and began to read to himself. It was from Deadra.

"Ross!" the officer called out, and again the letter was passed back. Jamel glanced at it briefly, and when he didn't recognize the sender, he passed it to Twan.

"Whooooa!" Twan let the excitement drag out

as he slowly opened the letter. At the same time he asked, "Whose letter you readin'? A secret admirer?" Jamel was too busy with his reading to answer.

Hi Darling,

　　Sorry we didn't get to spend a lot of time together on Sunday, but it was okay because we all got to see you. They're trying to break us up but that will never happen. All I can think of is one word, ENVY. Did you know that before we left the visiting room we were asked to be strip searched? We refused. Their reason was that they suspected something was going on. BULLSHIT! I feel very insulted and disgusted. I will talk to you when I see you on Monday, the 12th. I was worried when you didn't call me when we got home. I hope to God that you are okay. By the way, how was your softball game that evening? I hope your team won. I will send you some money in a few days. I will always be yours. JoJo will always be yours. Your children love you.

Love Forever,
Deadra and JoJo

　　P.S. Do you think I should get my lawyer?

\- \- \- \-

At the same time, Twan was quiet as a mouse, reading the "secret admirer letter" Jamel had handed to him. Roy looked over Twan's shoulder.

> *Jamel,*
>
> *I found out about you through a friend. Never did I think I would be writing to a brother I don't know. As I write this letter, however, there is a big smile on my face. I just appreciate what a man you are. I heard you are into music, poetry, and reading. I also heard you've been having a little difficulty where you're at. But regardless, I know you're standing strong and doing what has to be done. And in case you need a lil' something to get you by, just know that you have a good friend . . . a secret admirer who cares about you.*
>
> *Your Secret Admirer*

"Ooo-wee!" Twan said. "Miss Secret Admirer!"

Jamel snatched it from him. "Lemme see that." He scanned it over, but didn't give it a second thought. After all, real women—even if they were in jail—were sending him all kinds of letters with promises galore. Name

included. What did he want with a person afraid to use
their name?

"Ross!"

Jamel,

*How are you doing? Fine, I hope. Me, I'm
fine. It's always a pleasure to hear from you. We
are in the process of writing you another short
story—something for Father's Day maybe? Stay
tuned! I copied and passed on your information
to a number of other women here, so you don't
have to worry about getting spread. (Smile) Nah
mean? My girl Brenda and I will be handlin' our
business. Speaking of Brenda, she is always very
complimentary of you. I remember her once telling
me, "Now that's the kind of man I need to always
have in my corner." She's always talking about how
intelligent you are; how successful, but yet humble
you are. She is sending your info to some women
at the institution in Michigan. We joked about
keeping you to ourselves, but we were only joking.
(Smile) Brenda said that you're too wonderful to
be selfish with. She also said some other things (all
good) but, yes, that's strictly girl talk. I also wanted*

*to say that I'm glad to have met you and know
that you're there for me. Thank you. Thank you for
your hugs, too. I sure needed that. I'm also glad
to hear your fellow convicts are happy. Anything
to keep the brothers strong and to pass time. I'm
here if you need me, okay? Well, I hate to close,
but I have to go. You take care and continue to be
that strong black man that you are! Peace, much
respect, and much love,*

Tammy

"Ross!"

Greetings Mr. Jamel Ross,

*I apologize for the delay in writing. Actually there
was a little misunderstanding about who should write
who. I wrote to one young man there at Fort Dix, but
I think I may have been a little too direct, and too
much for him. As for you, Tammy said you would like
to hear from me. I can't understand why, because I
really don't think I'm your type. I'll let you decide.*

*There is something about you that I find quite
intriguing and that turns me on. On the other hand,
I didn't want to step on anyone's toes. So I wrote to*

the other guy I mentioned. Know that he was second choice. You've probably seen a photo of me by now, but I'll lay it out for you. I am twenty-eight years old, the epitome of a brick house, milk chocolate with beautiful bedroom eyes. To describe my character, I'd have to say I'm independent, strong-willed, confident, intelligent, direct, sensual, and affectionate. Basically, I'm the model Aquarius. My hobbies include sewing, reading, baking, dancing, sex, and traveling. I am single and have never been married. I like children but I don't have any of my own. I would like to adopt someday for I have no desire to give birth. I never thought very much of marriage because I've witnessed too many divorces. I am the oldest child of five, raised in a single-parent home. I learned responsibility at a young age, which could account for my bossiness at times. I left home at age twelve and became a stripper and escort. I became what is known as a dominatrix/mistress a year later. I still participate when the opportunity arises, which leads us to my being bisexual, for most women who participate in S&M are bisexual. Although I'm bi, I still believe in monogamy. I think any intimate relationship should be one-on-one, because there is no need for extra

*people . . . extra luggage. I think my sexuality is what
scares people, specifically men, but Bree is gonna be
Bree, regardless. I can't be fake and I won't accept
any flakiness. So now that you know a bit more about
me, what are you going to do with the info? Write? Or
hold off? The cards are in your hands.*

Brenda (aka Bree)

"So what are you gonna do, Jay?" asked Roy.

"Well, she's right when she says she's not my type.
But that monogamy stuff? That's for the birds. Two's
company and three's *mo' betta*," said Jamel.

"I hear that," said Gliss.

"Anyway, twenty-eight and she's a brick house?
I could probably deal with that. But she'll have to be
gentle."

The three others laughed their asses off.

Gliss said, "But I just don't know how a nigga like
me can't be down. *Dag*."

CHAPTER 13

If there's such a thing as the point of no return, when a woman decides in her mind, Yes, I'd go to bed with him, then indeed, Kay had reached that threshold. Up until Jamel was locked up in the hospital wing, before she got a full-on look at his fine chocolate self, practically in the buff, Kay had only learned what was in his mind. She read up on what details the government had documented about him and, to some degree, she could read him. But that day when he was behind the glass he was so thorough, so real. She could almost see below the surface, his healthy body and his good heart. He was such a romantic. He said words to make her warm and he shared ideas that had her open. Did he really mean it when he said he'd do anything for me? she wondered. Was he just saying that because he was locked up and backed up? Kay never had a man to do anything quite unique to or for her. There was the usual, sure. Flowers. A date for dinner. Movies. But what was unique about that? And why was Jay so different? She was curious about this bad boy.

In her bed, Kay gyrated against her pillows. She held a pillow between her legs and one in her embrace. She squeezed and squeezed, imagining him, wanting him. At one point she was shaking, feeling the pain that was set within her own harnessed desire. A feeling that had her breathing heavy while praying for relief to the God who watched over lonely hearts. What more could she do before she crossed the line and committed herself? She had made things easier for him, arranged for the two-man room. She reached out to him anonymously through a letter. What was next before she reached that point? Before she actually crossed that threshold?

■ ■ ■ ■

Every six months a dozen convicts are called into the unit office for a team review. The unit team was a group of staff members who generally reviewed a convict's behavior and progress on an individual basis; eventually everyone would have a turn. If everyone was present, the unit manager, the unit counselor, and the case manager all sat in on the review. However, at Fort Dix, with its limited staff—at times there was approximately one officer on duty for every two or three hundred convicts—it was not unusual for a case manager to run the six-month review alone, basically going over the checklist of goals achieved and goals projected: Have you completed any college courses? How about your community ties? Are you maintaining contact with your family? We suggest that you take up an adult continuing education course . . . any questions? Sign here. End of review.

In Jamel's unit, Ms. Cozza was the unit manager. She was popular for having turned in her husband for prohibited acts he committed as a staff member. Smartened by watching over ten years of convicts and knowing all about their backgrounds, their objectives, and even their habits had empowered Cozza with a know-it-all approach to things. Yet, with all that going for her, she was in a Weight Watchers rut, was predictably emotional, and still fell for men who were nonachievers so that she could keep the upper hand. Mr. Dillon was the unit counselor. A cocky-walking, clean-shaven ex-naval dropout, Dillon enjoyed imposing his authority in the smallest ways, no matter what lies he had to tell in order to earn the respect of the convicts of Unit 5852. But little did he know, his performance was see-through to the thorough convicts and his sexuality was constantly questioned in whispers. Dillon also found himself walking on eggshells from time to time due to the increasing complaints filed against him. Mr. Soto, the short, fragile one with the blue eyes and sometimes rebel haircut, was the one to play Mr. Nice Guy. He was the case manager whom convicts consulted with regarding their sentence calculations and their prison record. Although Soto was supposed to be exclusive to this concern, he often indulged in the counselor's role at will. In essence, the soft blue eyes were just a disguise: he was nice, but only to an extent.

Jamel was in a position to hold such opinions about the staff because 1) he watched them day to day, weighing their actions along with everyone else's. Did they observe patience? Did they maintain integrity? And 2) Jamel kept his ears and eyes open throughout his stay at Fort Dix. He was a walking talking recorder. His eyes provided video, his ears audio, and his mind took notes and stored data. Inasmuch as Ms. Cozza was the know-it-all of staff members, Jamel was becoming the know-it-all of convicts. He preferred to keep these six-month reviews quick and uneventful, but who said things always came up roses?

"It says here in your PSI that you are disturbed in terms of interpersonal relations, such as feelings of entitlement, exploitation, relationships that alternate between the extremes of overidealization and devaluation and lack of empathy. Do you think that you still have these problems? Should we suggest routine visits to the psychotherapist?" Jamel smirked, well aware of what the paperwork said about him.

"'Idealization'? Oh yes, I still have that problem. I still live in my own perfect world. And that's the way things will always be. And 'devaluation'? Do you mean I tend to keep others down so I can shine? Hmmm . . . you know, I'll have to admit that there was a time that certain people bothered me. If they didn't do things a certain way . . . the way that I thought they should be done? I'd think the worst of that person. Like if a person doesn't wash, or if their teeth are cruddy, or maybe their ideas are small and take very little effort to accomplish. I admit there was a time I frowned on such people. But over these past years, during this prison bid, my own ideals have changed. I believe this universe is balanced out. If there's good over here, then there has to be bad over there. That's just the way it is. So I'm a 'live and let live' guy, now. I mean, so what if you're overweight and have low aspirations? So what if you like men and can't help lying? And so what if you're a fake, a phony, and a fraud? It's all good to me. It won't change who I am and where I'm going . . ."

"Are you finished?" Ms. Cozza said, suddenly realizing that all three staff members had just been insulted.

"If *you're* finished," Jamel replied sarcastically.

■ ■ ■ ■

Box, Twan, and Roy were with Jamel, standing on line in the chow hall. The chow hall was similar to the cafeterias at Big Boy or White Castle or even McDonald's. Tile floors. Four-at-a-table seating. The service line and salad bar. The place had filled with over three hundred convicts, either eating or standing on line or working, and conversations buzzed throughout. To pass the time, Jamel had been detailing his team review.

"You said *that*?!" Box said, wide eyed.

"Why didn't I?" Jamel answered.

"Man, you got balls. What if they fuck you?"

"How? My date is my date comin'. Five months and I'm outta here!"

"What about halfway house? Don't you got that comin'?"

"Maybe. If they give me halfway house, I'll be outta here in two, maybe three months."

"Well, what if they fuck with that?" asked Roy.

"Roy, you know how I play it. When I go home, I go home. I ain't sweatin' no halfway house. That's just prison away from prison."

"Plus, dudes be comin' back from those joints every daggon week; like they like it here," said Twan.

"True. I figure a few extra months ain't gonna kill me. I did like five and a half already. I'm in a two-man room now. I'll just stay low-key, read, and brush up on my plans for the street."

"Yo, you still buildin' that club?"

"Am I? *Psssh* . . . man, just wait."

"Well, put me on, dog. I'ma be home in like five more joints, but hold me down."

"I got you, Roy. I might send a limo to pick your ass up."

Roy smiled and nodded, his eyes dreamy.

"What about your baby mommas? You still gonna be with them?"

"Well, they fucked up here and there, but I can't be mad at them. Nobody was really prepared for this. Not even me. They did the best they could, and they still brought up two healthy children."

"Yeah, dog . . . they did their thing all right. You gotta tighten that up when you get home."

"You better believe it."

"What about Tammy? You still gonna do the Jacuzzi thing with her?"

"I don't know. I mean, that was all good back then . . . when I was stressin'. But my shit is about to be on blast in a minute. You know that dude Bungy? Well, turns out he was the one to save my drawings—remember, the ones the cop didn't pack in my property? Back when I went to the lockup?"

"Yeah?"

"Maaan . . . quiet as it's kept, dude told me that if I kept it up, if I completed my planning, with the drawings and all, he knew where I could get funding. He promised to help me."

"Yeah, I believe it. They say white dude got long money."

"I don't know. I'm just stayin' focused. The pussy's gonna come. Gonna come rainin' down on me like champagne. But I'm tryin' to come up big so I don't never have to think about doin' illegal shit again. I got children now."

"True. Good luck, dog."

CHAPTER 14

The electronic message told the party on the receiving end to "press five to accept the call, and seventy-seven if you want to prevent future calls from the convict." Troy pressed 5 and the line was open for two-way communication.

"Yo! What's up, Jay!? I thought you'd *never* call. I gave my new number to JoJo like four weeks ago."

"Yeah, but they got some shit here where all numbers have to be approved and added to your phone list. It takes a while, especially if the staff drags their ass on it. So what's going on up in the BX?"

"Shit ain't the same since you left, Jay. Like three different magazines came out as soon as you left and all of them bit your style. And I know you heard about Mack and the trial."

"Yeah. We get cable 'n' stuff over here."

"Yo, *maaaann* . . . when all that shit was goin' down, I was like, 'Where is he!?' I wanted to talk to you so bad. That nigga was all over the press actin' like he's an angel, tellin' the world—"

"I heard it all."

"Yeah, but I wanted to reach through the TV and choke the *shit* outta that bitch-ass nigga! He had me hemmed up in the hospital for *six months*!"

"Yo, easy, dog. *Easy.* The main thing is you're alive and well now. You sound good as new."

"Yo, Jay . . . we can't let the shit go just like that. They just acquitted that punk ma'fucka for attempted murder, just 'cause he had money for a big-time lawyer. But still his homeboy didn't rat him out and got twenny years in jail. How far is he gonna go? How many people gotta die or go to jail before he pays?"

Jamel took a deep breath, unable to stop the images and pains of the past from seeping into his consciousness. Troy went on, "You weren't the one in the hospital on life support, Dee. I *was*! And still this nigga doin' videos 'n' shit, talkin 'bout he's 'still guilty, and still big willie.' That shit is killin' me slowly, dog. His arrogant ass is goin' down."

"Troy, Troy, *Troy*. Can we talk about that another time? I mean, I only get fifteen minutes on the phone."

"Oh, word?"

"Yeah. So I hear you had a son."

"He's beautiful, Jay."

"What's his name?"

"You ready for this? His name is Jamel-Troy Gates. I named him after you, dog."

"Damn, Troy. I ain't never had a kid named after me." Nobody could see this, but Jay was tearing up at the phone bank. "That's real, dog. That's *really* real. I'm feelin' a shiver just at the thought. *Psssh* . . . man. I don't know what to say."

"Can't wait for you to get out, Jay. You gave me guidance. You may not know this, but a number of people said I should stay away from you. They said you are bad, evil, and wicked. I heard it from people who were your acquaintances, co-workers, and 'friends.' People who dealt with you every day and hardly at all. They said it to the point of warning me. But I have always been aware of all or at least *most* of the things you have done. But I stayed loyal . . ."

Jamel was dumbfounded by these revelations. He was choked up and listening harder.

"You know why? I guess I was always inspired by you. No matter what you did, I saw you as a genius. Someone that I could learn from and just marvel at. The other reason is . . . you never did me wrong. Never did me dirty."

"Man. Sometimes when I look back, Troy, I can't ever remember hurting anyone intentionally. I was just focused. Ready to make money . . . tryin' to eat."

"Okay. But you know what else, Jay? I also sort of understand what makes Jamel Ross tick. There are different parts to you. There is a part of you that won't hurt me and another that will."

"Come on, Troy. You and I have been through hell together. Remember when we took that trip to Michigan? With fifteen performers on a luxury bus? We almost went off a cliff, dog! I still have nightmares about that."

"Me, too, Jay. Wow. From that day on, I never fell asleep at the wheel again. But Jay, I still hung with you. The one who everyone told me to stay away from. But you know what I always knew? From when we met, I knew there was some sort of connection. A *chemistry*. I even sensed you as a threat. But then I realized that we were sort of soul brothers . . ."

An electronic tone sounded on the phone. Jamel ignored it.

Troy said, "I hope I don't sound corny, but when you succeeded, I cheered. And when people hurt you, I felt pain. I saw so many qualities that I had, but that you had tenfold. Smart, creative, quick learner."

"You crazy, Troy."

"I'm serious, dog. Even our parenting is similar. I know you could never see it—no one does—but *trust me*! You were the aggressive tiger who destroyed anyone that dared to stop you from reaching your destiny. I was just the security guy. Muscles and skills. But I always knew if we could swap some of our stronger points within ourselves we would be pretty damn near perfect. And we were. Man, we did mad shows . . . mad accomplishments."

"I know. I think back and I go *wow!* We did that! It all just went by in a blur at the time."

"And fortunately we both survived it all. The good and bad. We're alive."

"But I just said that to you, fool!"

"I know, but that Mack shit gets me hot. When you comin' out?"

"Soon. I'll write to you. I think I'll need a ride home. I wanna surprise the girls."

"Aww, shit. It's about to go down in Yonkers."

"You better believe it's about to go down *everywhere*. If you think I was a monster before, wait'll I get home. I'm about to change the mothafuckin' game!"

- - - -

Two months passed before Kay posted an appointment on the institution's call-out for Jamel to stop by. It was the standard rule and all convicts were programmed to check the call-out sheet daily to find out if there was an appointment scheduled for the following day. Kay merely had to make the entry (which consisted of the convict's name and ID number) into her computer terminal and it would automatically be added to the call-out. If a convict missed a call-out, he was subject to an incident report, which begot penalties. This power that Kay had to call on convicts at will was something she held back on. She didn't want her boss, or the secretary, or other convicts to see Jamel coming around so often since everyone, including staff, had access to this universal bulletin. There would be talk. But now she was annoyed, because Jamel usually made the inquiry; but nothing had come across her desk in all this time. And almost desperately she needed to see him. Another option was for her to stop by 5852, Jamel's housing unit. But there was no justifiable excuse for that. And now it was she who wondered: Why doesn't he walk the compound like the others? Why doesn't he stop by? For now, all she had was the laser-printed photo of Jamel, the one from the BOP database. It was enough to keep Jamel's face in her thoughts.

On Thursday Kay learned that her boss and the secretary would be out that Friday. She was expected to "tend shop." It was the opportunity she'd been waiting for. She entered Convict Ross's name and ID number into her terminal for the next day's call-out. In the meantime, she took Jamel's picture home and stuck it on the bathroom mirror, the same mirror where she stood with her bare breasts and no makeup. Will he ever see me like this? she asked herself. Will he like it? Plain ol' me? Nothing enhanced or pushed up? Nothing hidden?

— — — —

Friday arrived in a foggy wrapper that made visibility minimal from even fifty feet away. So, as usual, Fort Dix remained shut down and the compound was closed except for the breakfast meal. An additional head count would need to be done and movement would be normal again once the fog lifted. This threw the entire morning off, because convicts neither went to work or to call-outs. Plus, there'd be less for the sentries to worry about—those white pickup trucks that constantly circled the perimeter, equipped with shotguns and shells in the event of attempted escapes.

The call-out that Kay had set up was for 8:00 a.m., so the appointment with Jamel Ross would have to be postponed until another day. But after lunch, the fog had long gone. And while some convicts used their half hour of liberty to exercise, to make phone calls, or attend to other errands, Jamel showed up to the psychology department anyway. Dr. Kay's door was locked when he got there, but he could see in through the narrow portal window in the door. Her office light glowed out into the darkened hallway so Jamel figured she was in and he knocked. Kay swung her head out of the office a moment later and when she recognized Jamel's face she smiled.

"Hi," she said after unlocking the door. "I was gonna reschedule you."

"Why? I'm here, aren't I?"

"Well, I guess so. Come on in . . . we're closed for the day so the lights are off. But we can chat a bit."

Jamel followed Kay into her office. He paid special attention to her backside, that unbelievably round ass of hers, well outlined by some navy blue slacks.

"Knickers?"

"Hmmm?"

"Aren't those called knickers?"

"Oh. My pants. Yeah, I guess. It shows off my lil' ankle bracelet. See?" Kay turned her leg just so to give her ankle attention. Jamel got an eyeful of her thigh, leg, calf, and, once he bent down, her ankle.

"Cute. A gift?"

"It says 'Daddy's girl.' My father gave it to me."

"Well, I suppose so. Who else would call you 'Daddy's girl'? Should I close the door?"

"It doesn't matter. I've locked the outside door. We're closed."

"And alone?"

"Ahhh, *yeah*," assured Kay.

"I was just wondering . . ." Jamel closed the door anyhow. Then he turned and approached Kay. ". . . if you could offer me some advice." He was feeling sure of himself right now. But, if he was wrong, his stuff was already packed back at the dorm; just in case he was dead wrong and Kay called in the goon squad to have him sent to SHU.

"Uhh . . . sure. What's up?" Kay folded her arms. But despite the defensive posture, her face said otherwise. She had a particular twist to her lips that men liked and she was crossing her legs slightly.

"I, ahh . . . know this woman. You could . . . you could call her my *secret admirer* . . ."

"Oh?"

"Yeah, I really didn't know her name, or where she knows *me* from. But then, the other night? I sat down and really, really took a long time to study just who this could be . . ." Jamel was a foot away, noticing Kay was about a half foot shorter than he. "Do you think you could help me find out . . . ?" He was now inches away, close enough to feel her stifled breathing.

"Who . . . ?" Jamel had backed Kay up to the rear of her office door. Her arms were helplessly at her sides when his lips connected with hers . . . when his hands cuddled her face . . . when his groin smooshed up against her body.

Jamel took it slow. He talked to himself the whole way through. This was the most sensitive moment of his life thus far. Even the brief deliberation at his sentencing (before the judge had given him all that time) wasn't as important as this moment. This was a space and time that was dictated by a throbbing heart and warped senses. Jamel applied great effort to not overdoing it. He'd been so far away from the promise of affection and companionship for so long he could've been a virgin. This touching and fondling, this closeness and the messages that her warmth was relaying to him were all so foreign. It felt crazy and at the same time exciting. It scared him and it turned him on. It was risky, yet he was growing ever erect.

Take it slow, Jamel, he told himself.

The newness of Kay's tongue tossing with his own was a taste he savored. His taste buds were numb against hers, lost in the want for more familiarity, the desire to be fed.

Kay did feed him. She probed as he did and she wrestled for depth as if inside the cave to his soul. She felt the need to hold him, and she did. Her arms felt natural around his waist and pulled him into her pelvis. She felt his hands wander and grip and knead her body through her knit pants and fluffy cashmere sweater. His hands caressed her breasts, cupping them as though they were dials of pleasure. His bulge was against her, instigating, encouraging, and frightening all at once. His breath was penetrating her pores, taking over the insides of her body. He didn't seem demanding or hasty and he didn't rush. Why did she hope that he might? Why did she wish for him to claw at her and pull at her as if latching onto his final breaths of life?

In the embrace, his natural fragrance, the intensity of his breathing, and the electricity that his body heat sent up her spine had both Kay's emotions and her consciousness fighting each other for control. She was spiraling—not inching, but diving deep into a pool of breathless pleasure. At the moment, you couldn't get a straight answer from Kay, even if you'd asked her name.

"What's your birthday?" Jamel asked right out of the blue. No warning, no soft sell, just a sudden question surfacing like a beach ball from the deep sea.

"Huh?" Kay murmured and sighed at once.

"Your birthday? What's your *birthday*?"

"May . . ." Kay's answer seemed to drift, her eyes wide open but dizzy. "May first." The words dragged from her mouth.

"A Taurus, huh?"

"Yeah," Kay replied, still lost in the meaning behind his eyes. Why did he stop kissing her?

Jamel could've read her mind. He was at it again, this time a little more aggressive, almost pressing her up against the door with his weight. His tongue reached around, making love inside of her mouth. Now Kay's eyes weren't the same as those of Dr. Kay the therapist. They were a high school cheerleader's eyes, the one who welcomed and fed into the energy of the young boy trying to score points. Only, even if the feeling was there, Kay was indeed an adult. They both were; it was just the activity that was youthful. They could've been in the back of a movie theater or in the backseat of a parent's car.

She was pulling him in again, wondering how far this would go and who exactly was in charge here.

"Okay, listen," said Jamel, collecting himself. "We gotta stop."

"If you say so," Kay replied, standing there against the door looking a mess; used like a rag doll. For a time, Jamel's hands were still on her breasts and he was still pressed there with his muscle snuggled comfortably in the space that was her belly. He backed off, smoothing his hands down her side.

"If we don't, I'm gonna explode and there's gonna be a mess. Can we do this again?"

"I'd like to if the opportunity comes. But today was great because my co-workers are away till Monday."

"Really?" Jamel suddenly felt a bit freer instead of under the gun. "I didn't—" He didn't finish his sentence, just attacked her again. This time, he *did* have her against the door, pressing his erection against her as if to drill a hole. For a second, Kay's hands were wayward, suspended to the sides at a loss for a home or resting place. Then, as if to give up in the heat of the battle, Kay's hands swung down and around to grip Jamel's ass. All she did was fan this into more fire.

Again, Jamel massaged Kay's breasts, unable to get enough of how good this felt. What was next? How far could this go? How far did she *want* it to go? She's not saying no, Jamel thought, does she want the whole nine yards? Should I take her to the couch? To the floor? Who's in charge here, her or me? He realized that Kay liked this just as much as, if not more than, he did. So he peeled her hands from his backside and he replaced them on the bulge between them. Damn! He was rock hard. Her hand massaged him through his knit sweatsuit and he thought he'd died and gone to heaven. Or at least that he'd gotten a furlough from jail.

"Kay," Jamel said between kisses. "I want you."

"I want you, too, Jamel," she revealed. "But . . . I . . ."

"Say you had all of this planned and you didn't provide protection?" Jamel asked with both question and answer.

"No, I didn't. I mean, I didn't have it planned and I *don't* have protection." Jamel practically deflated at the thought. He was as short as shit—close to going home—short like Mini Me from the *Austin Powers* classics—and he couldn't afford mistakes now. Half of him wanted to say fuck it and take the pussy for all it was worth. The other half wanted to pull back and use his common sense. Think. But when in the fit of passion did anyone have the time or the mind-set to think?

Jamel set aside the discouraging thoughts and he pressed back into Kay, his hands groping and pleasing her. Her moans and heavy breathing were either an incredible, uncontrollable reaction to his affections or else Kay moonlighted as an amateur porno actress. Whichever the case, the sounds were driving Jamel through the roof.

CHAPTER 15

Dear Diary,

*Today is the first day we're meeting; the first day I'm
writing such thoughts. So Hi! I know a person should be
starting such an endeavor earlier in life, but as my mother
used to say—it's never too late. I also shouldn't be starting
out with the subject matter I'm about to write about—
sex—but if I don't put this down on paper, and if I don't
tell SOMEONE, I'm gonna bust. So, for all intents and
purposes, this diary is exclusively for my freakish ways.
The other me. Note: If my father ever finds this I will kill
myself . . . or else move to Africa and feed the starving
children for the rest of my life. I'd probably pick the latter,
'cause I'm such a pushover deep down. Speaking of deep,
OH MY GOD!*

Today it happened. It didn't happen the way I imagined it would (whatever does?), but at least there were moments. A convict I met with stepped over the line. He imposed himself (and APPLIED himself, I might add) and I turned to Silly Putty. We were together alone in my office, and I haven't the slightest idea how THAT happened (smile), but he pushed up on me and we kissed for what seemed like hours. He virtually ravaged me with his hands, lips, and tongue, and (MY GOD!) I loved it! Every fucking bit! Excuse my naughty mouth, I don't usually talk that way, but don't blame me. He just, er, took over. I did have a fantasy about this; I mean, I actually envisioned something like this. But in my dream I stopped the advance before it started. I said no, and kept the fantasy a fantasy. I kept my desires to myself and the wet dream a secret for me to know and nobody to find out. But I guess human nature? The loneliness? Or his super charming ways? I don't know. Whatever the case, I let it happen. He has always fascinated me to no end and his hands were so gentle, yet so aggressive. His body pressing against mine, all up against my office door, was naughty, risky, and powerful all at once. And then after a lot of kissing and fondling, he put his hands up under my blouse . . . he unclasped my bra . . . and my God! It never felt so incredible to have a man handle my breasts like he did. I can't remember the stuff I was saying, but I was talking a lot once he got to the breasts. I think I said "OH MY GOD" like a hundred times, and I could hardly swallow at one point when he put his mouth on my nipples. He eased me to the couch and ate at my breasts like a castaway. I think I screamed once or twice when he licked the undersides. So so bad of me.

Then (you haven't heard the last) while I was soaking wet between my legs, Jamel pulled me to the floor and commanded that I lay back and keep my arms extended back over my head. He began kissing my midsection and my navel (I felt a surge when he did that). He hinted that he'd go on, only if I kept my voice down. I promised but I lied. I was too busy shaking all over anyway. He worked my pants down to the ankles—I don't know how he managed that!—and he lifted my legs back almost to my head. Now I was so weak . . . like I'd surrendered the last bit of privacy I owned. I felt so exposed and manipulated. My ankles and feet were caught in the web of my pants and he ordered me to hold my ankles and not to let go. I was delirious now, but I can remember telling myself that he was dead wrong and that every ounce of mystique or any protective shield that I had tried to hide under as a woman at Fort Dix was now tossed aside . . . all for naught. SHIT! (Oops, sorry.)

I can honestly say to you that I don't remember the rest. NO! Bear with me, it's not that I don't wanna tell you or write it down, it's just that I blacked out when he put his mouth on my kitten. THIS, I have to tell you, was absolutely the first time anyone ever did that. Even my college boyfriend (you know, the long relationship I had with Derrick) never did that. It was like I was missing an entire world of satisfaction. Like a whole other part of me was left high and dry. But this man Jamel, who incidentally favors Derrick a whole lot, took me to the universe. I felt like he dived into the innermost walls of my body, tongue first. And as of this writing, the evening after, I'm still exhausted and spent.

Listen . . . I need a cigarette or something. I'll have to get back to you later.

Kay E.

- - - -

"ABSOLUTELY INCREDIBLE! Maybe an interview in the very near future!" The letter was short and sweet. Jamel received the risky, in-house mail two days later.

Derelict

The in-house mail usually came in a brown envelope and was marked with the convict's name and number. But while Jamel was expecting that this was yet another boring communication from the unit team, maybe some notification from his halfway house or another unit team review (they became more frequent once the convict got "shorter"), it was actually an unsigned note from Kay.

She's off the hook, Jamel told himself, sure that his buddies didn't get a peek at the letter.

"Some team shit?" Box asked.

"Mmm-hmm. Ain't shit," Jamel replied. But in his mind he knew he had that bitch open. She'd even written another secret admirer letter with all kinds of accolades; Jamel had to hold this one from the others, too.

Jamel,

First of all, let me just say how pleased and appreciative I was to receive (uhm) your letter. Yes, God has truly blessed me. I feel undeserving. I went out of my mind after your "letter." Shocked. But when it wore off, with me in a bathtub of scented crystals, I was suddenly empty. Oh! Don't get me wrong. You've filled me up (with your uhm, letter). Boy oh boy, did you fill me up. But I don't have you here with me to bathe together, to dine together, to share life together. That's the empty part. I'll have to really adjust and get used to this, for what? A few months? I've enjoyed a good life so far. I'm certain life ahead holds many promises for me. Aren't you one of them, darling? Won't I have you here to hold me and to take over like I know you can? I remember the formula you told me about once, how to set goals and objectives. It's obvious that through a lot of determination, motivation, and ambition one can do or have anything he/she chooses. You're a prime example of that. My goal is you, Jamel. And look where we are now . . . closer than close. More intimate than anyone could ever know.

By the way, I'm glad you're arrogant and bossy, because I find that arrogant men rarely ever lack self-confidence and are quite successful in any and all of their endeavors. I'm going to close for now, but not before I say that I'd like to reciprocate that "favor" you did for me (wink).

Thanks again. It's been real.

Love, your semi-secret admirer

"Listen, Box. Do me a favor and get the rest of my mail?"

"No problem. Where you goin'?"

"Up to my room. I need to look for somethin'," Jamel lied, just wanting to get away and be alone in his room. Almonte played dominoes all damn night, so there'd be plenty of privacy. Plenty enough for Jamel to take his time with Kay's letter. He wanted to allow his erection to build without a whole bunch of nosy men around. He wasn't sure if he read the letter right: Promises? One of her promises? I'm her goal? Those things bothered him. No erection there. But she said he "filled her up," that she was "glad" he was arrogant and that she wanted to "reciprocate" the favor he did for her. By those statements, Jamel could grow like a tree—a solid oak. He read those parts over and over, and he enjoyed the sensation that pushed through him in the meantime.

With the letter laid on the bed beside him, Jamel recalled the moments in Kay's office. It made a major difference to his bid to have a form of release. To be able to have another woman—no matter who it was—to touch him as she did. To kiss him as Kay did. He was so reckless with her, eating his way to her very soul. One minute it was Dr. Kay Edmondson, and the next, it was just another bitch on the floor with half-assed looks getting her pussy eaten good 'n' plenty.

Jamel was proud of himself. Proud to be a slut and to have plenty of experience satisfying women. A lot of men talked of never going down on a woman: "A pimp don't do that," Joe Black would say. "You go down on a bitch and she got yo' ass pussy whipped. Her slave," Naiim would say. And Jamel didn't wanna even guess what the *asalam alacum* dudes might have to say about eating pussy.

But Jamel knew different. Any woman he ever knew who had this privilege of his tongue between her walls (and that wasn't everyone) was one he had for life. She wouldn't leave unless told to; it certainly wouldn't be by her *own* will. Deadra told Jamel that JoJo didn't even do it as good as he did. JoJo said virtually the same thing about Deadra. These mentions stimulated Jamel to no end on the phone (and he'd never share what one said about the other), if only to build his ego and assure himself that he was that inexpendable presence in their lives. As far as Jamel was concerned, Kay didn't experience life until he'd gone "downtown" on her. And just as he'd guessed, now she was hooked. The way it looked, whenever the opportunity presented itself, Jamel could go over to her office, have her block up the window, and he could get his dick sucked by an amateur. And Jamel knew that amateurs were the best; he could do the teaching and in that way whatever he said would go. Jamel couldn't wait to see Kay again. Hell, the way he was going, he didn't have to fuck her, he could get his shit off—maybe he could even get her to swallow—and in a few months he'd leave all of this behind. All of it, even the psych.

CHAPTER 16

The ghetto girls came out in legions with their over-size earrings, their bare midsections, navels showing under tube tops, and hot pants that covered none but the genitalia. Their hairstyles were off the hook, too; weaved, braided up, finger waved, glittered, and shaped. All of these women and some guys, too, latched on to Mack the very second he swaggered onto MTV's *Total Request Live*. Some were affixed to his mere celebrity. Others were more involved, taking note of his uniquely crooked teeth, his braids pulled back into a ponytail, and his glistening suit bright enough to steal attention from the sun. Fans were waving pictures of Mack. These were the same diehards that glued their ears to the radio and their eyes to their MTV just to smell "the Mack." And that was also the title of his forthcoming album, his second so far.

The first album hit triple platinum thanks to the army of popular artists and producers who joined in to ride Mack's coattails. Meanwhile, the cult he created was infectious and, thanks to the brute force of TV and radio, his image and his ideas spread throughout the world. The male fans dressed and talked like him and danced like him. The female fans, mostly young impressionable schoolgirls, had nothing better to do than fawn over him and suck up to the image he portrayed. The diamonds on his cross. The platinum medallion. The outfits that hypnotized them. They obsessed over every move and gesture of the ghetto fabo's private and public life. Wannabes galore. And there didn't seem to be an end to it.

Mack had, maybe, just as many haters out in the world. They called him fake. A homo thug. And they built and developed their own fans for the dozen-plus "I hate Mack" websites. The haters were made well aware of the Mack's past, how he grew as a promoter of haphazard parties, where partiers were maimed in fights and where concertgoers were trampled to death because of penny-wise and dollar-foolish security provisions. Mack had no concern for anyone else's life, or even the victims that resulted, so long as he made his money. The websites said it all, with all the eyewitness accounts and police reports; all of it at the click of the mouse. The graphics that were submitted to these websites, with their claims of hundreds of thousands of page views per week, had photos that were altered to show the worst side of Mack. There was Mack the transvestite, where an ingenious graphic designer added makeup, eyelashes, and platform shoes to the publicity photo. There was Mack the ghost, wherein a student created an image complete with powdered face and gloomy outline. And there was the all-popular Mack the devil, wherein some brilliant designer added fangs, horns, reddened eyes, and a tail with an arrow that whipped up and under to symbolize a thin red pointy penis. All of these photos were now viral, as web surfers e-mailed one another with the stories, the photos, and the testimonies. For real, there was a cancer of hate overshadowing the Mack's forthcoming album.

Troy absorbed it all, and was as involved as a hungry pit bull, planted there in front of his TV. For sure, he had long succumbed to the rage in his heart. Just as

Mack's interview began, teasing the television audience about an album due out in a few months, Troy, with perspiration on his brow and shaking like he was, lifted up the 45-caliber handgun to blast three shots off at his own television screen. The unit helplessly short-circuited, some bright muffled explosions went off inside of its walls, and smoke wafted above the toppled wreck of glass, plastic, and electronic components.

"*Mothafucka*. Your ass is grass."

CHAPTER 17

Can't hold me, can't fold me
You jive turkeys will never ever get to know me
You only hate me because you can't be me,
Wrists blingin', ching-chingin' like a money tree . . .

You spend your energy hatin' on a real G
You mothafuckas is so blinded that you can't see
That I'm a staple in this hip-hop community
So many hits that Sammy Sosa can't see me . . .

Jamel and Roy were in the weight room, a section of the building that made up the Fort Dix recreation department. Roy had a wide frame. He was just inches shorter than Jamel but his muscles, not just his chest and arms either, were all probably three times larger than Jay's meager beginnings. Jamel guessed that Roy was born that way, and maybe 50 percent of the results were due to his own power and discipline. Regardless, the larger convict was a leader and a disciple both. He looked up to Jay's passion and personal power, while Jamel looked up to Roy's rock-solid integrity, as well as his physical power.

For now, Roy was spotting Jamel, who was lying on the incline bench, pushing ninety-five-pound dumbbells for the third set of five repetitions.

"Come on! Gimme that money! Get it! Don't you hear that song up there? That's your buddy—the Mack! *Get it up!*" The beats continued to fill the room. Jamel got mad and fumed. The dumbbells were three quarters of the way extended but the tough talk and the image of Mack on TV took him over the top. A sudden surge of energy helped Jay to get the weights all the way up until his arms were extended for the full stretch.

"Good money," Roy said, the cue for Jamel to drop the weights to the rubber-matted floor. They bounced by his side. He jumped up and took heavy breaths, feeling the adrenaline reaching his head, the anger mixing with the feeling of accomplishment. All of those contradictions were swimming inside of him as he flashed the awkward expression at Roy, his hands on his hips.

Roy's response was, "Don't get mad at me, that's *your* issue. Use it as positive energy. Get mad. Make it burn. By the time you hit the shower, you'll be rid of that punk."

"Yeah, but tomorrow they'll be playing his song on the radio again. You'll be sayin' some ol' dumb shit again."

"*Yup.* And the mothafucka ain't gonna go away, neither. Not until you clear your mind. Not until you let it go."

"It ain't that easy, dog."

"They say, 'Let go, and let God.'"

"Yeah, but God wasn't there that night dude ambushed us."

"Sure he was. There's a reason for everything."

"I just can't get all the way with that God stuff, Roy. I mean, when it comes down to it, I'm a believer. I can't front on the miracles that we have in our faces every day. But sometimes I think God—if there is one—is sleepin' on some of us. All the tragedies from day to day. Kids gettin' shot. Terrible car accidents. World hunger. AIDS. How could God allow so much pain and misery and, on the other hand, promise life after death?"

"It's complicated, dog, I know. You just have to have faith."

"Faith." Jamel grunted. "I have faith in *me*, right after oxygen and water; right after the sun and moon. Now stop stallin' and get my money," Jamel said, pointing at the weights.

— — — —

A month of secret admirer letters went by. Jamel nearly overdosed on music videos, making it a routine to work on his business plan and sketches from midnight to 6:00 a.m. Breakfast was at 6:05. He'd sleep at 6:30, half-conscious of the various live radio interviews playing in his Walkman headphones, and he'd get up at 11:30 to watch a *106 & Park* rerun. He'd play a couple hours of chess over lunch, then there was four o'clock count, mail call, dinner, and his job sign-in. After a shower, Jamel was back to bed to catch up on sleep and to wind up for another long night at work.

Once a month there were staff meetings that left a "skeleton staff" to oversee the 1,500-plus convicts. A secretary might even fill in. Most every activity on the compound, even the call-outs, was canceled when these meetings came up. At approximately 1:00 p.m., a convict recall was announced over the institution's PA system. All convicts knew to return to their units.

The monthlong wait was killing Jamel. He constantly replayed the events that took place in Kay's office. He couldn't get that damn ankle bracelet out of his mind, how it dangled there with the whole "Daddy's girl" inscription, as he engrossed himself in the trip down to her nether regions. As a memento of the brief engagement, Jamel had even taken Kay's soiled panties back to the unit with him. She advised against it, warning that if an officer found them Jay could get in deep trouble; trouble that she might not be able to bail him out of. Jamel demanded, however, and at that point, as relieved as she was, already weak with satisfaction, Kay couldn't argue.

And the panties came in handy during the month of separation. They still had her scent and Jamel's primal desires were aroused at the slightest whiff. To add fuel to the crackling fire, Kay was consistent with the letters. He wondered if she'd ever run out of stamps, perfume, and lipstick as much as she wrote him:

So what are you doing over there? I'm trying hard not to appear thirsty (smile). I immediately needed to communicate with you. One thing I'm certain of is that as long as our lines of communication stay open, I can do this time along with you. I can free your mind and satisfy you. Confession time: I dream about you so much. Over and over again. And it's so strange how much impact you have on me. Thank you, Jamel. Thank you so very much.

Another letter said,

Every time I look at your photo, I want to put on my space suit, for these are the moments I find myself walking on the moon. You are far too incredible! Before I go any further, happy belated birthday. I knew something about you was rare and extraordinary. Capricorn. Born for success. So tell me, the reason you purposely made me wait to receive a letter from you is because you wanted me to die of

*thirst over here. Oh, how inhumane of you . . . oh Jay,
you can't know how much I look forward to seeing
you. It's been far too long a wait.*

Yet another letter said,

*Guess what? By the time you receive this letter I will
have completed a 30-day meatless diet. Remember,
in one of our conversations, you were telling me
how you deleted meat from your diet for over 10
years? Well, this is something I've wanted to do for
a long time. If only you could have entered my life
a lot sooner, I'm sure a lot of things would've been
different. Everything happens at its appropriate
time, huh? I'm a changed woman because of
you . . . I refuse limitations and replace them with
determination. It finally sank in that this is my time;
time to persevere without hesitation. Go for it! It's all
about you and me, boo. When you get out, I'm gonna
make a life for you and me that is like none other.
Those street chicks you once loved will be the last
thing on your mind because I will be your everything.
Since you're my therapist, tell me how I'm supposed
to manage without you around? I need you. I guess it's*

*sort of obvious that I've had very few influential men
in my life. But I know you will change all of that . . .*

— — — —

Blah blah blah, Jamel thought. There was no question
in his mind that the woman was *open*. And he couldn't
wait to see her any longer.

At 3:00 p.m. the compound was opened briefly
for food service workers to report to the chow
hall and for the sickly to report to the "pill line" for
their next dosage of Thorazine, Motrin, or whatever it was those guys took for their ills. This was
the window of opportunity he needed. There was
no accounting for who went where for what during
that hour between 3:00 p.m. and 4:00 p.m. when the
traditional stand-up count was done. The unit secretary filled in anyhow and wasn't as familiar as the
usual officer with the everyday protocol. So Jamel
took off. By his estimates, he could make it down to
Psychology by 3:05. He'd hope to meet up with the
good doctor, handle his business, and by 3:30, 3:45
at the latest, he'd return to the unit for the 4:00 p.m.
count. Kay might not even be in her office, but it was
worth the effort.

The door to the building that housed Psychology was open. Jamel climbed two cases of steps in record time and knocked at the steel door. The lights were on.

Kay imagined that the secretary had come back from the staff meeting, and she immediately stopped what she was doing to scoot to the door. Jamel's smug smile on the other side of the rectangular window was a treat to see, as if a river of joy suddenly washed through her. She wasted no time in letting him in.

"How did you manage this? I thought there was a recall!"

"There was, but I know the Fort Dix system like the back of my hand. I just had enough time to stop and see you."

"Oh?"

"Let's step into my office, shall we?" Jamel said this as if it were true. He didn't crack a smile. Intrigued, Kay followed him. She didn't bother locking the door since the compound, and certainly the building, was virtually a ghost town.

The minute Jamel stepped in, and she behind him, the embrace was romantic. The hungry kissing and frenzied hand work ensued. Jamel pulled away briefly, talking to Kay amidst the action.

"I . . . got your . . . letters. So you've . . . been miss-ing me, have you?"

Kay was flooded with emotions, passions, and lust. She wanted this man in every way and more. So engrossed was she that she had to ask him to repeat himself.

"Huh?" she replied to the words that passed over her.

"I said, I think it's time for some of that reciproca-tion you talked about in one of your letters."

"Oh." Kay stopped and gave that some thought. Then she held Jamel close, cradling her face against his collarbone and neck. It was the moment she needed to collect herself. She'd imagined this over and over again in her dreams, how she would eventually give him back what he'd given her—and more—but it hadn't quite played out this way in her sleep. In the dream, it was Kay who did the initiating, wherein she'd surprise Jamel. But now she was content to submit to his desires. His wish was her command.

"I had a surprise for you," Kay mentioned, as if it were too late.

"Yeah? Better hurry. It'll be 'recall' soon."

"I've been . . . *preparing* for this," Kay said, unable to establish eye contact with him. A little bashful.

"Really? Tell me more."

"I rented a few tapes."

"What tapes?"

"Heather Hunter this. Heather Hunter that."

"You're *lying*," said Jamel with a deep laugh.

"No. I'm telling you the *truth*. I watched the videos— all of them, start to finish."

"And what do you think, ahh, *doctor*? Does Heather need help or what?"

"I don't really think so. She seems happy with what she does. *Very* happy."

Jamel kept his tongue, not wanting to let on to his awareness.

"So I took notes on, you know, the *reciprocation*."

"Okay. You mean like pencil-and-paper–type notes?"

"No. Just *remembered* certain things."

"Okay. So you think you've got it down?"

"I'll do my best."

"Alrighty then. Let's get to the part . . ." He kissed her neck and eventually spoke directly into her ear. " . . . about you on the carpet. Think you can put those knees to work, baby?"

"Mmmmph . . ." Kay moaned. "Demanding, are we?"

"Hey, listen, we don't have the time, Kay. Now

let's make this happen. Get on your knees for me. Lemme see just how real you can keep it."

"All right, all right, but take it easy. This is, you know, a *first*. How about some sensitivity?"

Jamel didn't want to blow this. He knew this woman inside-out as the therapist, but he also knew that women were always subject to change their minds. He was quiet now as Kay eased down, first to the couch, then one knee at a time until she was on the floor beneath him. It was too quiet as Kay worked Jay's sweatpants down over his erection. So just to fill the air, Jamel spoke.

"So how did you prepare?"

"I practiced with bananas and whipped cream."

"Wow. You *did* practice."

"It was a little messy, but after three bananas I got the hang of it."

"I'll be the judge of that."

"Judging me now?" Kay's eyes smarted along with her tone.

Jamel had about enough of the challenges. As far as he was concerned, he got past that part when he put this woman on her back. When he had her begging him to "keep going." Now Jamel put his palm against Kay's cheek in a master/slave hold.

"Would I judge you, baby? The woman of my *dreams*? The focus of my days and nights? You're turning out to be everything I ever *wanted* in a woman. The early start of my new life? I guess I'm just stuck with being arrogant and bossy. Will you forgive me?"

In response to Jamel's words, Kay's face changed to compassion, then determination.

"This time has beat me up."

"I'll do even more than that," Kay promised.

"More than beat me up?"

"No. More than *forgive* you."

Jamel was fully erect now and Kay was handling him with two hands, the way he liked it. It was exciting to realize how easy it was to get over on this so-called therapist. All he had to do was say certain things, just some words, and she was moved from fear and wonder to confidence and assurance. He stood there as he had done on many occasions in the past, as if he was positioned in front of a urinal, with his hand on his hip and the other in her hair, combing through it possessively. When she finally took him in her mouth, his head tilted back with his eyes closed and his mind delirious. It had been over a half decade since his dick had felt the slithery tongue of a woman. It was as if he'd come home. He'd *finally* come home.

After a time, with Kay's gurgling sound effects intoxicating his senses, Jamel opened his eyes to watch her. Her eyes were closed and she was so much into the act. Within no time, he was caught between exploding in her mouth and not, wanting this to last forever; and if not *that* long then at *least* till 3:45. Five years of backed-up, stopped-up, pent-up passion was held up inside of him like a dam about to burst. Like a volcano about to erupt. Deep into the act, with Kay pulling and pushing at his foreskin, Jamel came to realize that he'd reached that threshold. Kay was now his missionary, his slave, and his sex toy. And in prison, he realized that her having gone this far meant she'd do just about anything else, so long as he willed it into existence. What would she do now if he were to flip on her? If he were to go hard with her and treat her like the bitch he dreamed of and not the lover he fooled her into believing she was?

Those thoughts alone made the spasms push through him and he blasted his semen in her mouth with total abandon. He didn't hold back, just kept shooting his juice inside of her jaws to gag and swallow and almost choke on. When he did, Kay's hands became suspended at a loss for what to do.

"Suck it, baby. Show me you love it. Go 'head. *Suck it*." Jamel the demon.

Kay's eyes beckoned as they peered up at Jamel. He could see his semen oozing down the sides of her mouth as he tried to maintain composure. His legs practically buckled under him. Jamel was spent and Kay was used. It was the way it was supposed to be. It was the way it was.

"Oh shit," Jamel said, noticing the digital clock on Kay's desk. "It's four o'clock." As fast as he could, he pulled up his sweats, patted Kay on her head, and hightailed it out of her office.

"Just tell them . . ." Kay started to yell, but then figured she could just as well make a phone call and tell the unit officer that the convict was with her in a sensitive conference. A life or death head case, she might tell the officer. After all, she was recognized as an officer, too, so why would anyone doubt her word?

— — — —

Jamel took great strides down the steps to the first floor. He pushed through the stairwell door and then pulled at the next door that led to the corridor out of the building.

"Hey! Where are *you* going? It's recall."

"I was . . ." Jamel was pointing and talking, but the officer was closed to excuses.

"What time is count time?" asked the officer with that condescending tone.

"Four p.m., sir."

"They called recall over fifteen minutes ago. Why are you late? Let me see your ID."

"I was"—Jamel was reaching into his pocket for the prison's copycat ATM card, complete with his photo and black magnetic strip—"upstairs. Psychology department," he said, trying to catch his breath.

The officer looked over the ID before turning his eyes to Jamel.

"Better hurry," the officer said. And Jamel nodded, vaguely recalling the cop working in laundry services.

"Thank you. Thank you," Jamel said on his way out the door and up the compound.

— — — —

Kay was adjusting her bra when Joe Steel stepped through Psychology's entrance. She could hear keys and hurried to straighten her clothing, her hair.

"Oh, Joe. Hi."

"Hi, *yourself*. Was Convict Ross up here?"

"Ah . . . yes, as a matter of fact we just finished up . . . running late, you know."

"Oh. Business as usual?" Joe asked as he canvassed Kay's office with his curious eyes.

"Sure. Think I should call his unit officer?"

"No. I did that already."

"Oh. Thank you."

"Some funny business going on here?" Joe asked, picking up Kay's hairpin from the carpet.

"Excuse me?"

"The hairpin. Your chin."

Kay was horrified. She bent down to pick up the pin and at the same time pulled her sleeve across her chin. Her eyes avoiding a connection with Joe's as she said, "What brings you up here, Joe?"

"Actually I was just double-checking doors, Kay. But here I see a convict running from your office, out of bounds, and you're up here with some . . . what's that? Semen *on your mouth*?"

Kay had turned her back and was behind her desk now, her hand wiping her chin.

"Joe, you have *some nerve* making inferences like that. I'm a *professional*."

"I bet you are. *I bet you are*. So this is why you've been avoiding me. For a goddamn *convict*? I'm pushed to the side by Convict Ross, huh? Is that how you play me?"

"Joe, you're jumping to conclusions. First of all, you're wrong about the convict, and second, you and I had a date. *That's it*. Nothing more, nothing less."

"So what, I wasn't good enough for you? What do I need—a prisoner's ID and registration number?"

"Joe!"

"No, Kay! You ain't no woman. You's a two-bit ho."

Kay stood with her hands on her hips. Swallowing. There was a silence. Joe read Kay's face. *Guilty.*

"I'm gonna write that punk up for being out of bounds. See if I can't mess up his out date like he messed up my chances with you."

"Joe, you're being silly. And you're wrong about Ross."

"Good. Then you shouldn't care either way if I write him up. Policy is policy, ya know." Joe turned to leave Kay's office.

"Wait. Joe, *wait!*" Kay made strides and had the officer's elbow in her grip within seconds. "Joe, don't do this. Please."

"Oh! So there *is* something going on here. Some freak shit, huh? Don't do this? Please?"

"Joe . . ." Kay's head dropped. "Please."

"Please *what*?"

"Please don't, don't write him up."

"And what do I get? What's it worth to you?"

A tear fell from Kay's eye. She was suddenly trapped. Her job might be on the line. Jay's freedom might be jeopardized. Her career. Kay didn't know what to do. She could've shrunk right there. Disappeared even.

"What do you want from me, Joe?"

"Well . . . you wouldn't go out with me. So maybe . . . maybe you could give me some of what Ross got."

"Fuck you." Kay sneered.

"No. Fuck you. And fuck *him*!" Joe was back on his way out of the door, headed down the carpet. Then he heard Kay and said, "What was that?"

"I said I'll do what you want," she repeated.

"Aw . . . why do you have to be so sad about it, babe?" said Joe the CO with phony compassion. "Just think of me as another one of the boys. And besides . . . this shouldn't take long . . ." He loosened his belt. "I'm a one-minute man."

CHAPTER 18

"**H**ey, Deadra, I'm glad you're home. How's everybody?" Jamel was snuggled up in the corner phone bank, using what was left of his three hundred minutes per month.

"We were just talking about you, boo; going over things we'll be doing and places we'll be going when you get home. JoJo and I both worked and chipped in for a big gift for you. I know you'll like it. Plus, we're planning a little shopping spree for you, ya know, for clothes and stuff. We should have like twenty grand for that alone . . ."

"Wow, you guys are really doin' good. What's the catch?"

"Oh, stop it. You put up with the big-time sacrifices for us. You took a fall and now we're here to help you bounce back."

"I don't know what to say."

"Don't say shit, babe. Just sit back and enjoy the ride we're gonna be givin' you. We were *just* sayin' how you're gonna be a virgin when you get home."

"Yeah. I guess so."

"So we're gonna pop that cherry, baby."

"I don't know, maybe I'll just settle for being *your* sex slave. *Your* loyal servant, with all these good things you're planning for me."

"You mean you're not gonna be sayin', 'Bitch, suck my dick'? Like before?"

"Probably not. I'm a nice boy now. A changed man."

"Yeah, right. Here . . . JoJo wants to talk to you . . ."

"Hi, boo! Jay, I miss your ass so much. Did they give you a date yet? Do you know when you're coming home? I know it's close."

"Real close, boo. Just keep it tight for me and I'll be there to take care of business."

"If your business gets any tighter, babe, it's gonna dry up like a prune. Hey, someone wants to talk to you."

"Hi, Daddy!"

"Sonia! How's Daddy's lil' girl?"

"Fine."

"I miss you."

"I miss you, too, Daddy."

"And I love you."

"I love you, too, Daddy."

"You been looking up at the moon and the stars and thinking about me?"

"I saw the moon the other night, Daddy, and I told Mommy you were up there."

"Oh! That's so beautiful. You're such a beautiful little girl."

"Thank you, Daddy. Daddy, you wanna speak to Jamel?"

"Sure, baby. Give Daddy a big kiss." She did. "Okay, put your brother on."

"Daddy!"

"Hi, Son. Have you been studying your rules?"

"Yes, Daddy."

"Okay, what's rule number eight?"

"Uhm, 'good times and bad times are all *the best of times.*'"

"Number six."

"'Today is the happiest day of my life, because I have strength, courage, and enthusiasm.'"

"Okay! Here's an easy one. Tell me rule number one."

"'Be good to others and they will be good to me.'"

"Wow, Jamel, you make me so proud."

"Thank you, Daddy. Mommy says you're coming home in a few weeks."

"That's right, Son. And you remember what I promised you?"

"Disney World!"

"That's right. And what else?"

"Fishing! And horseback riding!"

"Bingo."

"Roger that."

"Where'd you hear that, Jamel?"

"*Rambo*."

"Okay. Time to put Mommy on."

"Hey, babe."

"Boo . . . what'd I tell you about violent movies and the children?"

"Baby, we do our best. But sometimes we slip."

"I'm gonna slip my foot in your ass. Can you for once do as I ask? No violent movies for the kids. And that's final."

"All right, baby."

"I won't have to say this again?"

"No, baby."

Then Jamel said, "No, Daddy," expecting his woman to repeat after him.

"No, Daddy, you won't have to say it again."

"Okay. You all be good. Gimme a kiss." Deadra did. Then JoJo did. And Jamel hung up.

— — — —

Jamel became glued to the music videos in his final days at Fort Dix. It was the tension-relieving activity that he reserved especially for this time in his incarceration. He just couldn't get enough of the tits and asses that danced across the television screen. Within that TV box was the perfect world, the convenience of easy sex and of his fantasies come true. As far as Jamel was concerned, he'd paid his dues. He did the time; it didn't do him. He had the fights, endured through the stressful hours and sleepless nights, and it had all served to toughen his Teflon. He was through with the pen pals, the communal living, the floor buffing and the jailhouse lawyers, the random shakedowns, the arguments over the TV, the phone, and over who had more money, Puff Daddy or Master P. He was tired of the unit team with their lying, scheming, bleach-white attitudes and the bias through which they saw all men. He was done with powdered food and canned food, and grimy shower stalls and all the many odors of men. He was done with the squiggly channel and four-foot gangsters. He was done with Kay; done turning her out. She served him well, and now it was finally over. Jamel was going home.

CHAPTER 19

That day with Jamel and then Joe put Kay over the edge. She was smoking now. She put in for sick leave and used the time to live out her depression. She'd never felt so used in her life. Furthermore, she couldn't rid herself of Joe's face, an image that popped up in her sleep, his scent still fresh on her mind, and how she vomited immediately after he'd ejaculated in her mouth. He was so nasty tasting, and it had served him right that she'd thrown up on his pants. That was the only thought, the only spiteful image that helped her keep her sanity. Kay was sure that Jamel didn't know what she'd done. And it was best that way. She just needed time away, time to pull herself out of a rut. She wasn't sure how to face Joe if she ever had the chance to see him on the job. Did he tell anyone? Would he gloat when he saw her? Was Jamel still leaving prison on time, with no incident?

There was so much to think about. So many concerns. Enough to make her drag from the Newports all day long. Maybe another visit to the diary, or another secret admirer letter to Jamel. No. She didn't have the desire. Not in the mood to write a long letter.

Dear Jay,
   I miss you.

Always,
K

CHAPTER 20

The day had come. October 1st, 2003. Six years of misery behind him and a beautiful autumn sky ahead of him with freedom in its wings.

"Remember what I told you, Jay. You stay out of here for six months, you follow your plans as you've laid them out for me, and I'll see that you get the money you need to make your club happen."

"Okay, Mr. Bungy. Thanks for all the advice." Jamel was being extra nice in parting, already familiar with parting promises, those eleventh-hour convictions. Ordinarily the promises came from the one leaving, not the one left behind. But to Jamel, it didn't matter much anyway. He'd go for what he wanted and he'd get it just as with anything else in his life. If Bungy didn't come up off of that money he was said to have banked away, it was no big deal. Jamel had more pressing concerns: his loved ones and getting adjusted to life in the streets. Business used to come first. It was second now. There was time enough to stop and smell the roses.

Box, Roy, and Twan still had a total of twenty-two years to serve, but they had been by Jamel's side for most of his six years in prison. Now they were strolling beside him, taking that short walk with him to the R&D building and hoping for some of liberty's traces to rub off on them.

"I got a gift for you, Twan."

"Yeah? Well, Jay, one thing for sure and two things for certain, I sure love gifts."

Jamel knew Twan was gonna do ten years more than the rest of his buddies. Furthermore, Fort Dix had recently imposed a ban on girlie books or anything with explicit photos. Even *Playboy* wasn't allowed anymore. So, needless to say, the forthcoming years wouldn't be pretty.

"Just because I know how you love to smell the coochie, Twan." Jamel pulled the soiled panties from his bag and tossed them to Twan.

"Whoa!" Twan said and he took a nice long whiff before stuffing them in his pocket. At the same time, Box and Roy laughed hard and loud.

"Roy, you watch out for those dudes that say they're gangstas, but who snivel about the smallest, most unimportant things known to man. And Box? Gangsta boo and Kelly Twice ain't worth the effort, dog. If them COs let you hit it, even if they tag team your ass, it might be your last spin. Take my word, you'll be sorry."

After the chuckles, the guys said their good-byes. Jamel was processed through R&D and he glided out through the front lobby of the administration building. It was as easy to leave, he realized, as it had been to come in. Only this time he felt all the weight and burden lift from his shoulders. Ten years younger and he would've kissed the pavement or clicked his heels in the air. But this was a man leaving. And there were many more important things to do.

■ ■ ■ ■

Troy was out there waiting in the truck, a brand-new model of the Land Rover. It was mint green and had a complementary mint scent inside.

"I did it," said Jamel, feeling somehow that he'd gotten away with murder.

"'Sup, Jay!" Troy said as his longtime friend got in the truck. "You all right?"

"Hardly. You see that fence, Troy? A lot of misery inside there. Men with thousands of years to serve. So much wasted time and energy. And you know what they argue about in there?"

"Tell me."

"The TV; the mothafuckin' TV. Shit that costs a few dollars out here, somethin' that represents a tiny percentage of what a person lives, and it's *everything* to them in there. I actually heard dudes proclaiming a TV as their own. *'My TV!'* Fuckin' sad. No grip on life, years just passing through their fingers and no accomplishments to show for it."

Troy didn't know if he should respond, so he just kept it quiet.

"Drive, dog. Just drive," Jamel said with his bitter memories hanging over them.

■ ■ ■ ■

The long strip of road that leads from Fort Dix passes McGuire Air Force Base and its airport where planes—

big, gray, military types—fly in and out every few minutes. Troy didn't hear the commotion at first even
though there was a plane passing overhead. But once
the engines were out of earshot and the planes out of
sight and the vibrations of both faded away, the car horn
*toot-toot-toot*ing behind the Land Rover was audible.

"Somebody's trying to get our attention, Jay;
headlights and all." Jamel turned around in his seat to
see a compact Honda Accord following a car length
behind them.

"Slow down. I wanna—" Jamel got a better look.
"Oh *shit!* I thought she forgot about me."

"Who? What's up?"

"Pull over, dog. Lemme talk to this bitch, see
what's on her mind."

"You need me?"

"Not at all. I got this."

It was no more than a minute and a half later when
Jamel returned to the truck.

"Troy . . . do me a favor."

"Anything, just ask."

"About a mile down there's a motel. Trenton
Arms, she says."

"What's up?"

"Just drive. I'll fill you in along the way."

In the parking lot of the motel the Land Rover was parked a couple of cars away from the Honda. Kay Edmondson had already gone into the motel's front office to rent a room for a day.

"So that's the whole story," Jamel explained. "I just need to tap this one time real good. You know, just put my pimp down to scare her off. And I'll never hear from her again."

"I feel ya. Well, I'll be honest, I wish I could watch."

"Trust me. The bitch ain't much to look at. Considering where I've been and the women I've seen in my life, she's probably a two."

"Well, then, *do you*, dog."

"I intend to. There she is. Put me on the clock, cuz this shit won't take fifteen minutes."

— — — —

Kay was a bit nervous. She'd never done this before, either—the whole quickie-in-the-motel bit. But her job and her home were here in Jersey and Jamel had to go to New York—he had seventy-two hours to check in with his probation officer, blah blah blah. All Kay knew was that this was the day she'd been waiting for.

A good-looking, AIDS-free, success-oriented black man who, although he had his faults, she wanted to spend quality time with. The man she wanted to love and hold. And she wanted for him to love and hold her. It's what she'd dreamed about every night and day for all these months. It's what she could've lost her job for. It's what she sucked some other man's dick to preserve. Jamel Ross. Ex-con. Bad boy. And damn, it'd been a long time since the day he ate her kat.

Jamel leapt out of the truck and went into room 126, not two steps after Kay went in. When the door closed she turned to him.

"*Finally.*"

"Yeah. Finally."

"You don't seem so excited," said Kay.

"Oh, *believe me*, I'm excited. I've also got a real busy schedule today, babe. So let's do this."

Kay was already approaching him. She missed his soft kisses, his aggressive hands, and his warm body. No, he hadn't been inside her yet . . . not as a man was built to enter a woman, but she hoped he'd be inside her today.

Kay was the one to pull away. "What's up?" Jamel asked.

"I gotta go to the lil' girls' room," she said in a little girl's voice. It obviously turned Jamel on.

"Before you do that, I want you to do something for me." Jamel looked behind him. There was a chair against the wall. He took it, turned it around, and sat with his arms relaxed on its back. Kay was there in front of him, mere feet away. "Back up a little." She did. "Turn around and lemme see you."

"But . . ." Kay had a strange look on her face.

"Ahh, just do as I ask, sweetheart. This is *my* fantasy we're living out here."

"Well, okay," she said in a saucy voice. She did a slow turn. An amateur's move.

"Take off your clothes."

"Right here?"

"Right there. Take 'em off, and *listen*—please do it fast," Jamel told her. But to himself, he said, Do it fast because we've got the motor running outside. Kay began to strip. The knee-length skirt. The blouse. The bra. The panties and stockings. "No, no, leave the pumps on, baby."

"Ooooh, particular, *huh?*"

"Yeah, *real* particular. So you still need to go to the ladies' room?"

Kay nodded.

"Gotta wee-wee?"

Kay nodded along with that cute teenager's guilt.

"Go ahead then." Kay spun to run to the bathroom.

"Uh-uh, don't leave. I want you to go right here."

"Here, baby? On the *carpet?*"

"Did I *stutter*, Kay? You said—and I quote—'I will do anything for you, Jamel.' Did you not say that?" Jamel gave her no room to respond. He simply said, "Spread your legs like those double-oh-seven whores do in the movies." Jamel felt her stalling and he put his arms up, as if to say, "What are you waiting for?" Kay broke out of her guilt with a smile, and that's when Jamel knew he had her lock, stock, and barrel.

"That's it, spread 'em. Put your hands on your hips—go on. Now, throw your head back, think of me, and let it rain."

"I don't . . . *baby!* I don't think I can do it—it's so *uncomfortable.*"

"So then you don't really have to go."

"Oh, but I *do*. I really do."

"So then let it go, baby. *Do that shit.*"

Kay took a deep breath, bracing herself for another new event. Already she had crossed the line between sanity and Jamel's wild imagination. So, she figured, what else is new? She encouraged herself to go for it and tilted her head back and squealed. The stream of pee shot down to the floor below her, glazing her calves and soaking the carpet between her feet. She squealed some more.

"Oh my *God*," she exclaimed.

"How you like it? Feel good?"

"Feels hot and crazy, baby. This is *bananas*!"

"I'm sure." Jamel grew an erection that was stiffer than wood. It seemed that after this, there was no end to the things she'd do for him. All he had to do was ask. "You done?"

"To say the least. But can you tell me why?"

"Nah. Better that things are left unsaid." He got up from the chair, walked over to the small, swampy carpet, and kissed her. "Okay, baby. You know the routine. Get down on your knees for me."

"In the *pee*?? On my *knees*?"

"*Fuck*. I swear there's an echo in here." He kissed her again. Then he whispered in her ear. "It's sterile, baby. Ain't nothin' gonna hurt you. Now let's get freaky, and get on the floor and suck it," Jamel said with the cocky, urinal stance and the twisted gaze. His whisper tickled her mind and made her skin tingle.

∎ ∎ ∎ ∎

Troy didn't expect Jamel to keep with the fifteen-minute wait, but when he emerged from the motel room alone, Troy checked the time and curiosity showed all over his face.

"*Damn.* Twelve minutes? What'd you do, a hit-and-run?"

"*Basically.* Let's roll out." Jamel never looked back.

∎ ∎ ∎ ∎

By 3:00 p.m. the day of Jamel's release, he and Troy were sitting in the Land Rover for a talk. They were waiting to surprise Deadra, JoJo, and the children at their new apartment in the Riverview, a fourth-floor residence complete with three bedrooms, a doorman, and a broad view of the Hudson River and its New Jersey skyline. Jamel heard a lot about his new home and the girls even sent him photos. And they made him proud to see how complete, how comfortable, and how secure his children's home was. Sure, he had been away a long time, almost like being shipped off to war or sent into a six-year exile, and no, they didn't give him all six months of the halfway house program to help make his return easier. He just got three months. But despite those huge challenges, at least his children were well off. At least they had a roof over their heads and were protected.

"By the way, where did you get this truck? This is a *bad* whip. You must be doin' big things, Troy."

"I got news for you, Jay. This ain't my truck. It's yours."

"Man, *stop it.*"

"I'm serious. I didn't tell the girls where I was going, just told them I had to buy a gift for you and that I needed the truck to pick it up. They would've been suspicious, except they were so busy getting the kids ready for school when I came over this morning."

Jamel was suddenly looking over the SUV's interior with a proprietary interest.

"They both worked to get you this. Their credit, cash, the whole bit. I helped 'em pick it up two weeks ago."

Nodding with a tight grimace, Jamel was overwhelmed and choked up.

"You all really looked out. Thanks, Troy."

"Come on, *man*. I told you, we're like blood brothers. And there's somethin' else. Check under your seat."

Jamel reached underneath, grabbing something hard, and he pulled it out.

"*Whoa!* Troy, what's this for?"

Jamel was handling an M-16 assault rifle. He'd mastered this very type of weapon as a recruit in the military before he'd dropped out early. Still, he'd earned a sharpshooter's score by age eighteen.

"Unfinished business. Somethin' we don't need to talk too much about . . . just somethin' we need to *take care of.*"

"Damn, Troy. Me and guns are a big no-no. Ex-felons can't have 'em."

"Shit, ain't no sense in gettin' paranoid. I know dudes with more than four felony convictions, and they still keep an arsenal at the house. It's just a fact of life today, Jay. If you in the hood, *you gotta pack.*"

Jamel said nothing but his silence spoke loud.

Troy went on to say, "Just sit back and think a minute. You, me, and Roscoe, racing from a posse of Mack's 'follow-mes.' About five vehicles all loaded down with wannabe thugs. Guns blazin', adrenaline rushin', all of a sudden—*bam!* Beatdown. Me on life support. You, a month in the hospital. Scars. Pain. Nightmares. Stitches."

Troy was looking straight ahead, his eyes not paying attention to the life beyond the windshield. There were joggers, women with baby carriages, kids with their book bags, traffic, some loving couples. He saw none of this, only pain and misery caused by Mack years earlier.

"We gotta handle this, dog. You and me; *right now*. We're like ghosts sitting here. We don't exist. Your children are fatherless and your women are heartbroken. They couldn't even have open caskets for our loved ones to get a last look. We were too broken for the eye to see. Unfinished business, dog. *Unfinished business*."

TURN THE PAGE FOR EXCERPTS
OF MORE G UNIT BOOKS
by 50 Cent

BLOW

by 50 Cent
and K'wan

> "The game is not for the faint of heart,
> and if you choose to play it,
> you better damn well understand the rules."

Prince sat in the stiff wooden chair totally numb. The tailored Armani suit he had been so proud of when he dropped two grand on it now felt like a straitjacket. He spared a glance at his lawyer who was going over his notes with a worried expression on his face. The young black man had fought the good fight, but in the end it would be in God's hands.

He tried to keep from looking over his shoulder, but he couldn't help it. There was no sign of Sticks, which didn't surprise him. For killing a police officer they were surely going to give him the needle, if he even survived being captured. The police had dragged the river but never found a body. Everyone thought Sticks was dead, but Stone said otherwise. Sticks was his twin, and he would know better than anyone else if he was gone. Prince hoped that Stone was right and wished his friend well wherever fate carried him.

Marisol sat two rows behind him, with Mommy at her side looking every bit of the concerned grandmother. It was hard to believe that she was the embodiment of death, cloaked in kindness. This was the first time he had seen Mommy since his incarceration, but Marisol had been there every day for the seven weeks the trial had gone on. She tried to stay strong for her man, but he could tell that the ordeal was breaking her down. Cano had sent word through her that he would be taken care of, but Prince didn't want to be taken care of; he wanted to be free.

Keisha sat in the last row, quietly sobbing. She had raised the most hell when the bulls hit, even managing to get herself tossed into jail for obstruction of justice. She had always been a down bitch, and he respected her for it.

Assembled in the courtroom were many faces. Some were friends, but most were people from the neighborhood that just came to be nosy. No matter their motive the sheer number would look good on his part in the eyes of the jury, at least that was what his lawyer had told him. The way the trial seemed to be going, he seriously doubted it at that point.

Lined up to his left were his longtime friends, Daddy-O and Stone. Daddy-O's face was solemn. His dress shirt was pinned up at the shoulder covering the stump where his left arm used to be. It was just one more debt that he owed Diego that he'd never be able to collect on. Stone smirked at a doodling he had done on his legal pad. Prince wasn't sure if he didn't understand the charges they were facing or just didn't care. Knowing Stone, it was probably the latter. He had long ago re-signed himself to the fact that he was born into the game and would die in it.

Prince wanted to break down every time he thought how his run as a boss had ended. To see men that you had grown to love like family take the stand and try to snatch your life to save their own was a feeling that he wouldn't wish on anyone. *No man above the team* was the vow that they had all taken, but in the end only a few kept to it. To the rest, they were just words. They had laughed, cried, smoked weed, and got pussy together, but when the time came to stand like men they laid down like bitches. These men had been like his brothers, but that was before the money came into the picture.

CHAPTER 1
6 months earlier

"**C**ome on, Daddy-O, you know me." The young man reminded him, not believing that he'd been turned down. He could already feel the sweat trickling down his back and didn't know how much longer he could hold out.

Daddy-O popped a handful of sunflower seeds in his mouth. He expertly extracted the seeds using only his tongue and let the shells tumble around in his mouth until he could feel the salty bite. "My dude, why are you even talking to me about this; holla at my young boy," he nodded at Danny.

"Daddy, you know how this little nigga is; he

wouldn't let his mama go for a short, so you know I ain't getting a play."

"Get yo money right and we won't have a problem," Danny told him, and went back to watching the block.

"Listen." The young man turned back to Daddy-O. A thin film of sweat had begun to form on his nose. "All I got is ten dollars on me, but I need at least two to get me to the social security building in the morning. Do me this solid, and I swear I'll get you right when my check comes through."

Daddy-O looked over at Danny, who was giving the kid the once-over. He was short and thin with braids that snaked down the back of his neck. Danny had one of those funny faces. It was kind of like he looked old, but young at the same time . . . if that makes sense.

There was a time when Danny seemed like he had a bright future ahead of him. Though he wasn't the smartest of their little unit, he was a natural at sports. Danny played basketball for Cardinal Hayes High School and was one of the better players on the team. His jump shot needed a little fine-tuning, but he had a mean handle. Danny was notorious for embarrassing his opponents with his wicked crossover. Sports was supposed to be Danny's ticket out, but as most naïve young men did, he chose Hell over Heaven.

For as talented as Danny was physically, he was borderline retarded mentally. Of course not in a literal sense, but his actions made him the most dimwitted of the crew. While his school chums were content to play the role of gangstas and watch the game from afar, Danny had to be in the thick of it. It was his fascination with the game that caused him to drop out of school in his senior year to pursue his dreams of being a *real nigga*, or a real nigga's sidekick. Danny was a yes-man to the boss, and under the boss is where he would earn his stripes. He didn't really have the heart of a soldier, but he was connected to some stand-up dudes, which provided him with a veil of protection. The hood knew that if you fucked with Danny, you'd have to fuck with his team.

"Give it to him, D," Daddy-O finally said.

Danny looked like he wanted to say something, but a stern look from Daddy-O hushed him. Dipping his hand into the back of his pants, Danny fished around until he found what he was looking for. Grumbling, he handed the young man a small bag of crack.

The young man examined the bag and saw that it was mostly flake and powder. "Man, this ain't nothing but some shake."

"Beggars can't be choosers; take that shit and bounce," Danny spat.

"Yo, shorty you be on some bullshit," the young man said to Danny. There was a hint of anger in his voice, but he knew better than to get stupid. "One day you're gonna have to come from behind Prince and Daddy-O's skirts and handle your own business."

"Go ahead wit that shit, man," Daddy-O said, cracking another seed.

"No disrespect to you, Daddy-O, but shorty got a big mouth. He be coming at niggaz sideways, and it's only on the strength of y'all that nobody ain't rocked him yet."

"Yo, go head wit all that *rocking* shit, niggaz know where I be," Danny said, trying to sound confident. In all truthfulness, he was nervous. He loved the rush of being in the hood with Daddy-O and the team, but didn't care for the bullshit that came with it. Anybody who's ever spent a day on the streets knows that the law of the land more often than not is violence. If you weren't ready to defend your claim, then you needed to be in the house watching UPN.

The young man's eyes burned into Danny's. "Imma see you later," he said, never taking his eyes off Danny as he backed away.

"I'll be right here," Danny said confidently. His voice was deep and stern, but his legs felt like spaghetti. If the kid had rushed him, Danny would have had no idea what to do. He would fight if forced, but it wasn't his first course of action. Only when the kid had disappeared down the path did he finally force himself to relax.

"Punk-ass nigga," Danny said, like he was 'bout that.

"Yo, why you always acting up?" Daddy-O asked.

"What you mean, son?" Danny replied, as if he hadn't just clowned the dude.

"Every time I turn around your ass is in some shit, and that ain't what's up."

Danny sucked his teeth. "Yo, son was trying to stunt on me, B. You know I can't have niggaz coming at my head that way."

"Coming at your head?" Daddy-O raised his eyebrow. "Nigga, he was short two dollars!"

"I'm saying—"

"Don't say nothing," Daddy-O cut him off. "We out here trying to get a dollar and you still on your schoolyard bullshit. You need to respect these streets if you gonna get money in them." Daddy-O stormed off leaving Danny there to ponder what he had said.

■

The intense heat from the night before had spilled over to join with the morning sun and punish anyone who didn't have air conditioning, which amounted to damn near the whole hood being outside. That morning the projects were a kaleidoscope of activity. People were drinking, having water fights, and just trying to sit as still as they could in the heat. Grills were set up in front of several buildings, sending smoke signals to the hungry inhabitants.

Daddy-O bopped across the courtyard between 875 and 865. He nodded to a few heads as he passed them, but didn't really stop to chat. It was too damn hot, and being a combination of fat and black made you a target for the sun's taunting rays. A girl wearing boy shorts and a tank top sat on the bench enjoying an ice-cream cone. She peeked at Daddy-O from behind her pink sunglasses and drew the tip of her tongue across the top of the ice cream.

"Umm, hmm," Daddy-O grumbled, rubbing his large belly. In the way of being attractive, Daddy-O wasn't much to look at. He was a five-eight brute with gorilla-like arms and a jaw that looked to be carved from stone. Cornrows snaked back over his large head and stopped just behind his ears. Though some joked that he had a face that only a mother could love, Daddy-O had swagger. His gear was always up, and he was swift with the gift of gab, earning him points with the ladies.

Everybody in the hood knew Daddy-O. He had lived in the Frederick Douglass Houses for over twelve years at that point. He and his mother had moved there when he was seven years old. Daddy-O had lived a number of places in his life, but no place ever felt like Douglass.

Daddy-O was about to head down the stairs toward 845 when he heard his name being called. He slowed, but didn't stop walking as he turned around. Shambling from 875 in his direction was a crackhead that they all knew as Shakes. She tried to strut in her faded high-heeled shoes, but it ended up as more of a walk-stumble. She was dressed in a black leotard that looked like it was crushing her small breasts. Shakes had been a'ight back in her day, but she didn't get the memo that losing eighty pounds and most of your front teeth killed your sex appeal.

"Daddy-O, let me holla at you for a minute," she half slurred. Shakes's eyes were wide and constantly scanning as if she was expecting someone to jump out on her. She stepped next to Daddy-O and whispered in his ear, "You holding?"

"You know better than that, ma. Go see my little man in the building," he said, in a pleasant tone. Most of the dealers in the neighborhood saw the crackheads as being something less than human and treated them as such, but not Daddy-O. Having watched his older brother and several of his other relatives succumb to one drug or another, Daddy-O understood it better than most. Cocaine and heroin were the elite of their line. Boy and Girl, as they were sometimes called, were God and Goddess to those foolish enough to be enticed by their lies. They had had the highest addiction rate, and the most cases of relapses. Daddy-O had learned early that a well-known crackhead could be more valuable to you than a member of your team, if you knew how to use them.

"A'ight, baby, that's what it is." She turned to walk away and almost lost her balance. In true crackhead form, she righted herself and tried to strut even harder. "You need to call a sista sometime," she called over her shoulder.

Daddy-O shook his head. There wasn't a damn thing he could call Shakes but what she was, a corpse that didn't know it was dead yet. Daddy-O continued down the stairs and past the small playground. A group of kids were dancing around in the elephant-shaped sprinkler tossing water on each other. One of them ran up on Daddy-O with a half-filled bowl, but a quick threat of an ass whipping sent the kid back to douse one of his friends with the water. Stopping to exchange greetings with a Puerto Rican girl he knew, Daddy-O disappeared inside the bowels of 845.

HARLEM HEAT

by 50 Cent
and Mark
Anthony

Fast Forward to September 2006
Long Island, New York

J can't front. I was nervous as hell.

My heart was thumping a mile a minute, like it was about to jump outta my chest. The same goddamn state trooper had now been following us for more than three exits and I knew that it was just a matter of seconds before he was gonna turn on his lights and pull us over. So I put on my signal and switched lanes and prepared to exit the parkway, hoping that he would change his mind about stopping us.

"Chyna, what the fuck are you doing?" my moms asked me as she fidgeted in her seat.

"Ma, you know this nigga is gonna pull us over, so I'm just acting like I'm purposely exiting before he pulls us over. It'll be easier to play shit off if he does stop us."

"Chyna, I swear to God you gonna get us locked the fuck up. Just relax and drive!" my mother barked as she turned her head to look in the rearview mirror to confirm that the state trooper was still tailing us. She also reached to turn up the volume on the radio and then slumped in her seat a little bit, trying to relax.

Although my moms was trying to play shit cool, the truth was, I knew that she was just as nervous as I was.

"Ma, I already switched lanes, I gotta get off now or we'll look too suspicious," I explained over the loud R. Kelly and Snoop Dogg song that was coming from the speakers.

As soon as I switched lanes and attempted to make my way to the ramp of exit 13, the state trooper threw on his lights, signaling for me to pull over.

"Ain't this a bitch. Chyna, I told yo' ass."

"Ma, just chill," I barked, cutting my mother off. I was panicking and trying to think fast, and the last thing I needed was for my mother to be bitchin' with me.

"I got this. I'ma pull over and talk us outta this. Just follow my lead," I said with my heart pounding as I exited the parkway ramp and made my way onto Linden Boulevard before bringing the car to a complete stop.

I had my foot on the brake and both of my hands on the steering wheel. I inhaled and then exhaled very deeply before putting the car in park. I quickly exited the car, wearing my Cartier Aviator gold-rimmed shades to help mask my face. The loud R. Kelly chorus continued playing in the background.

"Officer, I'm sorry if I was speeding, but—"

"Miss, step away from the car and put your hands where I can see them," the lone state trooper shouted at me, interrupting my words. He was clutching his nine-millimeter handgun, that was still in its holster, and he cautiously approached me. Soon, I no longer heard the music coming from the car and I was guessing that my mother had turned it down so that she could try to listen to what the officer was saying.

"Put my hands on the car for what? Let me just explain where I'm going."

The officer wasn't trying to hear it, and he slammed me up against the hood of the car.

"I got a sick baby in the car. What the hell is wrong with you?" I screamed. I was purposely trying to be dramatic while squirming my body and resisting the officer's efforts to pat me down.

On the inside I was still shitting bricks and my heart was still racing a mile a minute. The car was in park at the side of the road and the engine was running idle. I was hoping that my mom would jump into the driver's seat and speed the hell off. There was no sense in both of us getting bagged. And from the looks of things, the aggressive officer didn't seem like he was in the mood for bullshit.

"Is anyone else in the car with you?" the cop asked me as he felt between my legs up to my crotch, checking for a weapon, even though he was clearly feeling for more than just a weapon.

My mother's BMW 745 that I was driving had limousine-style tints, and the state trooper couldn't fully see inside the car.

"Just my moms and my sick baby. Yo, on the real, for real, this is crazy. I ain't even do shit and you got me bent over and slammed up against the hood of the car feeling all on my pussy and shit! I got a sick baby that I'm trying to get to the hospital," I yelled while trying to fast-talk the cop. I sucked my teeth and gave him a bunch of eye-rolling and neck-twisting ghetto attitude.

"You didn't do shit? Well, if this is a BMW, then tell me why the fuck your plates are registered to a Honda Accord," the six-foot-four-inch drill-sergeant-looking officer screamed back at me.

The cop then reached to open up the driver's door, and just as he pulled the car door open, my moms opened her passenger door. She hadn't taken off the shades or the hat that she had been wearing, and with one foot on the ground and her other foot still inside the car she stood up and asked across the roof of the car if there was a problem.

"Chyna, you okay? What the fuck is going on, Officer?" my mother asked, sounding as if she was highly annoyed.

"Miss, I need you to step away from the car," the officer shouted at my mother.

"Step away from the car for what?" my moms yelled back with even more disgust in her voice.

"Ma, he on some bullshit. I told him that Nina is in the backseat sick as a damn dog and he still on this ol' racist profiling shit."

As soon as I was done saying those words I heard gunfire erupting.

Blaow. Blaow. Blaow. Blaow.

Instinctively I ducked for cover down near the wheel well, next to the car's twenty-two-inch chrome rims. And when I turned and attempted to see where the shots were coming from all I saw was the state trooper dropping to the ground. I turned and looked the other way and saw my mom's arms stretched across the roof of the BMW. She was holding her chrome thirty-eight revolver with both hands, ready to squeeze off some more rounds.

"Chyna, you aight?"

"Yeah, I'm good," I shouted back while still halfway crouched down near the tire.

"Well, get your ass in this car and let's bounce!" my moms screamed at me.

I got up off the ground from my kneeling stance and with my high-heeled Bottega Veneta boots I stepped over the bloody state trooper, who wasn't moving. He had been shot point-blank right between the eyes and he didn't look like he was breathing all that well, as blood spilled out of the side of his mouth.

Before I could fully get my ass planted on the cream-colored plush leather driver's seat my mom was hollering for me to hurry up and pull off.

"Drive this bitch, Chyna! I just shot a fucking cop! Drive!"

My mom's frantic yelling had scared my ten-month-old baby, who was strapped in her car seat in the back. So with my moms screaming for me to hurry up and drive away from the crime scene and with my startled baby crying and hitting high notes I put the car in drive and I screeched off, leaving the cop lying dead in the street.

If shit wasn't thick enough for me and my mom already, killing a state trooper had definitely just made things a whole lot thicker. I sped off doing about sixty miles an hour down a quiet residential street in Elmont, Long Island, just off of Linden Boulevard. My heart was thumping and although it was late afternoon on a bright and sunny summer weekday, I was desperately hoping that no eyewitnesses had seen what went down.